Ghosts
of the
Grand Canyon
Country

© James Wharton 2011

ISBN 1-57166-675-3

The reader should understand that we were able to obtain some of these stories only if we promised to obscure some of the actual identity of persons and/or property. This required us to occasionally use fictitious names. In such cases, the names of the people and/or the places are not to be confused with actual places or actual persons living or dead.

For my wife Carol
who inspired me to write,
and my mother Edna
for her wit and humor.

Table of Contents

Preface

Grand Canyon Country is an ancient, haunted land of spirits and secret places. Eerie wall paintings in remote inner canyons depict frightening spectral images, demons and other things that went bump in the night a thousand years before.

Long abandoned adobe buildings sheltered by massive rock overhangs tell of prehistoric civilizations forgotten by those who came so long ago they are now themselves forgotten.

Hikers are wise to stay on main trails for becoming lost in the maze of parched canyons and bewildering passageways risks cruel death.

A mile higher on the Canyon rims, ruined walls crumbled centuries before call out in unremembered tongues from other millenniums, voices of people long vanished from this ghostly place.

But one senses their presence and unexplainable things

in this mysterious land. Few dare speak of them. At day's end when the sounds of darkness begin, they listen for a bump in the night.

Sedona Picnic

Bitten by a rattlesnake, Letticia Wallace ran wildly through the rocky desert ravine. At first, she felt only a slight tingle and didn't realize the snake actually struck her. But as she ran, her ankle became swollen and the pain came. The running sped the circulation of her blood carrying the snake's poison making it hard to breathe and causing tightness in her chest The 4500 foot altitude of Sedona increased her breathing difficulty. Her blurred vision added to her anxiety.

Fun-loving and adventurous, "Lettie" was again in trouble because of those endearing traits. "I did everything wrong," she scolded herself, nearly collapsing as she stopped to rest on a rock. Her chest burned and body heaved as she gasped for air. "I got off the trail and lost track of where I was. Pull yourself together, Lettie."

While she had gotten into difficult situations before, eighteen-year-old Lettie realized she was in real trouble this time. She needed a doctor but was lost with no idea how to find the trail.

Earlier, Lettie, her father, uncle and aunt drove the 1908 Ford Model T west of Sedona for a picnic. It was early September in 1909 and Letticia Wallace had come to Sedona with her father for a visit with his brother Ned and his wife. The picnic site was a small park near a scenic overlook.

While the older people set up the picnic Lettie strolled across the footbridge leading to the trail and the overlook.

"Be careful, Lettie," her father yelled. "Don't go far."

"Don't worry father," she called. "I'll stay close."

Lettie had walked a hundred yards when she saw a cluster of bright yellow flowers next to three massive red boulders.

"They're perfect for a bouquet," she thought.

She finished quickly but as she began to re-trace her steps to return to the picnic, she was startled by a buzzing rattle and felt a burning feeling in her right ankle. She saw the snake slither into the brush to her left. The rattlesnake's fangs had penetrated the leather of her boot. Her immediate reaction had been to run as far and fast as she could.

But now, fearing for her life, she was sitting on the rock trying to figure out what to do. "Be calm," she told herself as she struggled to catch her breath. "Climb out of this ravine and find the trail, Lettie."

As she attempted to crawl up the steep side of the gorge, Lettie realized she was too weak. Suddenly dizzy, she fell to the ground. For a moment she glimpsed the clear blue sky and heard a fly buzzing nearby. Her eyes slowly closed as she fell into a deep sleep. Hours passed and the sun hovered low in the western sky.

Lettie thought she heard people talking but, still woozy, faded once again.

It seemed later when she heard the voices once more. Struggling to open her eyes, she could see the hazy outline of a woman's face.

"Who are you?" Lettie asked weakly.

The woman, apparently an Indian judging by her dark face and long black hair, smiled and pulled the cover up around Lettie's neck. Lettie's eyes closed again as she felt herself losing consciousness. Nightmares of being chased by monstrous snakes intruded on her sleep.

Lettie heard the muffled sound of movement near her. Still groggy, she managed to open her eyes to find the woman sitting next to her and smiling. But a man, also Indian, stood next to her. He looked strong and confident as he stood smiling at Lettie. She noticed he was very attractive.

"Who are you?" she asked.

"I am Lansa," the man answered. "You have been sleeping for many days. This is my Aunt Chu'mana. Her name means 'snake woman.' When our people have a snake bite, Chu'mana treats them. You are lucky I found you because the vultures were circling."

"You are not speaking my language," Lettie replied. "But, I understand what you are saying. How can that be?"

"This place is sacred," he said. "The Sky God lets us do things here that some consider magic, but they are his gifts. That is why we understand each other though we speak different languages. Rest now."

Chu'mana moved her hand over Lettie's eyes and she drifted into sleep. She awoke several times but dozed, then slowly drifted back into a sound sleep.

Lettie felt a tugging on her arm. "Wake up, Lettie," the voice said. Her eyes slowly opened and she recognized Lansa kneeling by her bed. She smiled, noticing his dark, intense eyes and reassuring smile. She wondered what it would be like to kiss him.

"Come with me," he said. "Chu'mana says you must walk now."

Lansa took her hand, helping her stand and walk through the doorway of the adobe building into the bright sunlight. Chu'mana smiled as they approached her. She was working on some kind of pottery.

"Chu'mana is making you a special gift," Lansa said. "It will be a bowl with beautiful designs on it. They watched as Chu'mana painted symbols onto a pot, an incredible work of art with black geometric designs over a white background.

"She does beautiful work," Lettie remarked.

Chu'mana smiled and paused for a moment, asking Lettie to paint something on the bowl. Not particularly artistic, Lettie painted her name in bold letters.

"I'm not an artist like you Chu'mana."

"That is alright," Chu'mana replied.

How long will it take for Chu'mana to finish the bowl?"

she asked Lansa.

"She is almost finished," he answered. "You may have it when you return."

Lansa took her hand and they strolled out of the village. Lettie turned to look back at the tan adobe buildings in the concave recess of the cliff wall.

"Where are we going?" Lettie asked.

"It's time for you to leave," he said sadly.

"What do you mean?" she asked. "I want to stay here with you."

"You cannot," Lansa said.

"I will come back tomorrow," she said.

"Yes, please come back. The pot will be waiting."

"I promise I will," Lettie replied, nodding.

They gazed at each other for a long moment before Lansa turned and walked away. He paused by a tree to look back and then he was gone.

Lettie hadn't realized Lansa had taken her to the main trail. She followed it for a few minutes and heard voices.

"Hello!" she cried out. "Is someone there?"

"Lettie! Is that you?" her father yelled.

"Yes, it's me, Father," she shouted.

Then she saw him running up the trail.

"Where have you been, Lettie?" Father asked excitedly. "We were so worried about you.

I can't believe you look so well after being in the wilderness for eight days."

"I didn't know I was gone that long, Father. But, I'm fine. Some Indian friends in the village cared for me."

As they drove toward town, Lettie described the Indian village and all that happened.

"There is no Indian village back there, Lettie," Uncle Ned interjected. "You are hallucinating from spending eight days exposed to the elements."

"Father, the Indian people took care of me after the rattlesnake bit me."

"Nonsense," replied Uncle Ned. "Nobody's lived back there for a thousand years."

"Ned," Father said, "I think Lettie is telling us what she thinks happened. But, I'd like the doctor to examine her."

"You think I might be imagining things, Father?" Lettie laughed.

"Possibly," her father answered laughing.

"Father, once the doctor checks me, can we go back to

the canyon?"

"Of course," he said.

The doctor confirmed a rattlesnake bit Lettie but, not believing her story, was amazed the wound healed without treatment. How was she alive after eight days without food or shelter?

"Young lady, he said, there is an archeologist in town who knows every Indian site within a hundred miles. Will you show him the people you met?"

The following day, Father, Uncle Ned, and the archeologist drove to the picnic site.

"The village where I stayed was built into a wall and was under a rock outcropping," Lettie said.

"I know that place. It's ahead on the trail," the archeologist replied.

A few minutes later Lettie yelled triumphantly, "There it is!"

"I have studied this site often," the archeologist said."

As they walked up the trail, Lettie's heart sank. The village was abandoned.

"There's no one here," she said.

"No one has lived here for a thousand years, said the

archeologist."

"But I saw them. They took care of me."

"Are you satisfied, Lettie?" Uncle Ned asked.

"No!" Lettie replied firmly. "I know what happened here. Do you believe me, Father?" she asked.

"Lettie, the doctor said you might be hallucinating because of the poison from the snake bite."

"But, how can I feel fine after eight days, Father?" Someone had to give me food and care for the rattlesnake bite. Otherwise, I'd be dead."

"We should go, Lettie," Father replied.

"Wait," Lettie pleaded. "Let me look around. Lansa told me to come back for a special bowl his aunt made."

"Lettie," Father said impatiently, "We came out here like you wanted. Please, let's go."

"Wait Father," she said. "Lansa promised the bowl would be here for me."

Suddenly she saw the outline of a bowl in the dusty soil.

"I found it!" screamed Lettie in excitement.

The archeologist ran toward her to help.

They carefully removed dirt from around the partially

buried bowl.

"Let me lift it out," the archeologist said, as he cradled the bowl in his hands.

"It is the most perfect piece of pottery I've ever seen," he said, as he handed the bowl to Lettie. "It's at least a thousand years old."

"My God!" Uncle Ned exclaimed, as he pointed at the bowl.

"What is it, Uncle Ned?" Lettie asked, alarmed at seeing his face turned completely pale.

"Look at the other side of the bowl, Lettie."

Father gasped as Lettie turned the bowl around.

Printed across its mid-section was the name "Lettie."

"I told you!" screamed Lettie excitedly.

"Yes, Lettie. You told us," Father said, obviously shocked.

"I painted my name on that bowl, Lettie said happily."

"That's impossible" the archeologist said. "This bowl is a thousand years old. These people had no written language."

Father smiled, aware something strange and unexplainable was happening.

"Lansa!" Lettie gasped, as she saw him walking toward them from the trees.

"I am Lansa," he said to the men. "Mr. Wallace, if Lettie chooses, may she come with me?

Father smiled and nodded. "Yes," he said, knowing, although not caring, that he had little choice in the matter. He could see Lettie's happiness and knew she must leave.

Lettie hugged her father and handed him the bowl. "You keep this for me father."

Holding hands, Lansa and Lettie turned and walked to the ancient cliff houses. They stopped to look back and wave then vanished into the building.

Visitors to the Palatki Historic Site near Sedona sometimes see a man and woman holding hands and walking through the thousand year old ruins. The two lovers are smiling and happy but when people approach, they mysteriously vanish. They seem to prefer being alone.

Prescott's Whiskey Row Ghost

"I killed him but I surely didn't mean to," Calvin Dupo sobbed as he began his weeping punctuated eulogy. "For them that don't know me, my name is Calvin Dupo, with a long "u" and long "o". I always think it's important to pronounce a person's name right. Don't you? We was usin' a noisy 1922 hay baler and Eddie said "no" but I thought he said "go" so I pulled the handle.

And poor Eddie got sucked into the hay baler and come out the other end all mixed in with that big, rectangular hay bale there. As you can plainly see, only his head is stickin' out the end of the bale. I mean, you go through one of them hay balers you don't come out the other end lookin' like you're ready for the Senior Prom. There ain't a coffin in the state big enough to hold Eddie and his hay bale body so he has to be displayed layin' across them two saw horses.

It was me that stuck them four broomsticks into the hay bale so Eddie would have arms and legs and look more natural. I bought the broomsticks and also them shoes of Eddie's over at the Dollar Deals Depot. You can get a real nice pair of shoes for a dollar.

Anyway, I rigged some blocks to hold the shoes in place so they'd stick upright and pointed at the ceiling. It wouldn't look right with Eddie in his hay bale body lying on his back and his shoes pointed toward the floor. That was somewhat artistic don't you think?

I also do chain saw art sculptures of large fish if you're ever in the market.

Eddie's wife Kay with a long 'a,' she put that pair of white work gloves on the ends of Eddie's broomstick arms. He always loved them white work gloves. After the funeral, Kay is going to put the broomsticks with the white gloves up in her front yard like they are wavin' to passersby. Eddie was friendly sometimes.

You woulda liked Eddie if you knew him good, though

he was at varied times mean as a snake and prone to fightin' and cussin'. He'd go down to them saloons on "Whiskey Row" and drink a lot and cause trouble. I wish he never died but not cause I don't care too much for dead people or that he still owes me ten dollars. I'm a little intoxicated but that don't affect nothin'. Think about it if your best friend went through a hay baler would you not imbibriate as well? Yeah, I would think you would. So don't stare at me in that demeanotory manner. Besides I don't like dead people so much. Did I say that already? But, other than havin' a bale of hay for a body, Eddie looks real good, don't he?

Oh, hi there Marge. For them that ain't aware, Marge is deaf in her left ear from the grain elevator explosion. She squints kind of odd unless you speak to her from an exact thirty-seven degree angle from the direction her head is pointed.

After the funeral the Mug Shot Tavern has Happy Hour prices on beer. It don't apply to premium beer cause the owner is formerly a convicted murderer but now a ex-convict who has some serious anti-social inclinations. I mean he don't discount premium beer cause it was so hard to get when he was in solitary confinement. Anyway I guess that makes it pretty easy to see where the Mug Shot got its name, don't it?

Oh, there's Kay, Eddie's old wife. I mean she ain't exactly old, she's just Eddie's old wife. I always say that don't I Kay?"

"Yes, you do Calvin, but you shouldn't tell that joke any more 'cause everybody in town has heard it at least ten times. Besides, I'm real tired of hearing it, Calvin."

"Alright Kay. Anyway, when the service is finished, we just have the six pall bearers stick their hay picks into the hay bale and carry Eddie to the cemetery.

My final comment concerns somethin' that happened late last night. And it was an awful thing. I dreamed that Eddie in his hay bale body and broomstick legs was in my bedroom standing next to my bed. He pointed his broomstick arm and white glove at me and screamed "You killed me Calvin!" And he kept screamin' it over and over. He was even wearin' them new shoes I bought him that are fixed onto his broomstick legs.

I went screamin' outta' my bedroom and out the front door. I run over to my ex-wife and her new husband's house and asked if I could sleep with them. Well, not like in the same bed but on the living room couch. Lucky for me they agreed.

In the morning her new husband and I went back to my house. It was then that I saw all them little pieces of hay on the floor right by my bed where I dreamed Eddie stood. But her new husband convinced me that the hay on the floor didn't fall off Eddie's hay bale body and was probably just a coincidence.

"But that's right where he was standing," I says.

"Don't worry about it, Calvin," he says. "Your house is so messy it probably come from your shoes."

"I hope he's right."

"Face it," he said. "Them broomstick legs ain't gonna support that big hay bale that is now Eddie."

"Yeah," I said, "and it rained last night and I read somewheres that ghosts don't go out in the rain."

He concurred.

"Oh no! Look at his shoes!" a woman shrieked from over by Eddie's hay bale body. "Look at his shoes!" came the hysterical scream once more. She was pointing at Eddie's new shoes on his broomstick legs. "They got mud all over them!" the woman shrieked. "Eddie was out walking in the rain last night!" she wailed, and ran for the door.

A stampede began as every one of the hundred plus

mourners pushed each other and cussed as they desperately tried to escape from the room all at once.

When things got settled down later, the funeral director went back into the parlor to take Eddie Haybale, as they now called him, to the cemetery. But, his body was gone. No one could ever figure out where it went.

But late at night when the last customers are leaving Whiskey Row in downtown Prescott, sometimes a man with a hay bale body and broomstick legs will chase after them. He waves his broomstick arms with white gloves and screams angrily at them, "You killed me, Calvin!"

The Phantom of Jacob Lake

"The eyes of death stared at me, a cold, heartless look that turned my soul to ice. I dared not meet his gaze, fearful of unleashing the evil of the man observing me."

That was the description given by Don Busby when he and his two ranch hands stopped for gas at the Jacob Lake General Store. As Don pumped gas into his new 1931 Ford closed cab pickup truck, the man approached him and asked for a ride.

Don considered himself to be a fair judge of character, and this man had an unnerving aura, which provoked a deep sense of foreboding. The man wore a black hat with round brim and his coal black hair was long and straight. His dark complexion and weathered face suggested he was middle age

31

and possibly an Indian but Don was not sure. The man's hard, unfriendly expression contrasted with his light denim shirt and faded blue jeans and jacket. His cowboy boots were well worn.

Although Don and his men wanted to reach Fredonia before nightfall, they had gotten a late start and it was nearly eight PM on this dark October night. They had come west past the Vermillion Cliffs on 89A and planned to follow it as it forked north thirty miles to Fredonia.

"Can I catch a lift?" the man asked.

Don smelled the strong odor of alcohol as the man spoke. "Which way you headed?" Don replied, mindful that 89A ran north and east and 67 ran straight south to the north rim of the Grand Canyon.

"I'm going north to Fredonia, friend," the man answered. "It's a cold night and there ain't many cars on the road." When the man spoke, his grim face demanded rather than invited reply, which he awaited in deathly silence.

"I'd like to help you out, partner, but we're headed east to Bitter Springs," Don lied instinctively. Although the man was also going to Fredonia, his intimidating appearance triggered some primal survival impulse in Don. He could tell by the fidgety demeanor of his two men that they too found this intruder unsettling. They had defensively moved to the opposite side of the truck on which they now leaned as they warily regarded the man.

Eerily, they sensed the man did not believe what Don told him. Bitter Springs was over fifty miles from Jacob Lake and there's nothing in-between or when you get there. Nobody would be travelling there this late at night. When Don refused to give him a ride, the man didn't answer. He icily apprised the three men and then, one by one, looked straight into the eyes of each man. His haunting, deathful glare sent chills up the men's spines. Silently, he turned and walked away.

"Let's get out of here, Don," one of his men said.

"You don't have to ask me twice," Don replied, as the three men scurried to get into the truck. As they slowly drove out of the gas station, Don looked back at the building. The man stood on the front porch under a dim light, carefully watching the truck as it rolled   toward the stop sign at the intersection of 89A and 67. Don stopped the truck and looked back again. The man's eyes were fixed on the men and the truck, carefully watching.

"He's still looking at us," Don told the men. "He's a scary devil. I wanted to get a cup of coffee but I couldn't stay around that guy another three seconds."

"You're telling me," the man next to him said. "He was spooky, scary."

Don turned the steering wheel to the left as he gradually let the clutch out while gently stepping on the gas pedal. As the truck rolled into the turn, he hesitantly looked back once more and was dismayed to see the man was still watching, following their every move. The left turn on 89A clearly signaled Don and the two men weren't driving east to Bitter Springs as he had told the fearful man. Instead, they were headed north by northwest, with nothing but pine forests between Jacob Lake and Fredonia.

That the man was also going to Fredonia stirred considerable unease within Don. The moonless, dark night and deserted road added to his anxiety.

"That guy gave me the creeps," one of the men said.

"I fought on the Western Front in 1918 and wasn't as scared then as I was seeing that fellow tonight," the second man said. "He seemed unearthly."

"Boys, I don't need to tell you he had me spooked. I can't get him out of my mind."

Over half an hour passed and they had almost reached

Fredonia.

"Don," one of his men said, "I could use a beer to calm my nerves."

"That creepy guy still bothering you?" Don answered.

"I'm afraid so," the man said.

"To tell you the truth, I can use a beer myself. I'm still thinking about that guy," Don replied.

During the entire trip, the tall pine trees on each side of the road seemed to intensify the darkness. They had not met a car coming south nor had anyone going north passed them. Don couldn't remember any other time he hadn't seen at least one car on 89A.

As they drove into the lighted outskirts of Fredonia, one of the hired men yelled, "Saloon!"

All three men laughed more loudly than the remark deserved, but it relieved the tension.

Don pulled into the empty parking lot and the three men climbed out of the truck and filed into the saloon. It was a weekday night and the dingy, poorly lit place was empty. As they walked toward a table in the back, they noticed only one person was sitting at the bar. His head was bent over his beer glass.

As the three travelers walked toward the man, he looked up and straight at them. The frightful man who had asked them for a ride forty-five minutes earlier now sat staring at the horrified men. Picking up his nearly empty glass of beer, he watched intently as they passed by.

Don led the way to a booth near the back of the bar. One of the men was visibly shaking.

"This is way too weird for me Don. Let's get out of here. How could he get here before us? We were flying up the road. Nobody passed us. How could he be here? "

"Calm down," Don replied, although he was not that calm himself. That the man had arrived before them was impossible. He was also at the bar long enough to drink a beer. There was no way this could happen. The waitress arrived at the table and, although both men wanted to leave, Don ordered three beers.

As the waitress turned to leave the table, Don said, "Oh Ma'am, just a moment!"

"Yes sir, what is it?" she asked as she turned back towards the three men.

"How long has that guy at the bar been here?" Don asked.

The waitress turned to look at the bar and then looked back at Don.

"What man at the bar?" she asked. "Are you trying to be funny? It's been a long night, mister and I don't need the jokes."

"That man sitting at the end of the bar with his back to us," replied Don irritably.

"Mister, are you nuts?" the waitress asked. There's nobody at the bar. You three are the only customers we've had in the last hour."

The three men looked towards the bar. The man was still there.

"Ma'am," one of Don's men asked, "don't you see that guy on the bar stool?"

It was then the waitress realized the three men at the table weren't playing a joke on her.

"Which chair is the man is sitting in," she said.

"It's the third stool from the end," Don said, impatiently.

The waitress, her face completely white, sat down in Don's chair. She looked like she was about to pass out.

"What's wrong?" he asked.

The waitress looked at him. "He's here," she said. "The Phantom of Jacob Lake.

"What do you mean?" he asked.

"Sometime back, people were being murdered by a serial killer in the area between Jacob Lake and Fredonia. Before he was captured, he killed over twenty people. The man's name was Frank Layton. Twelve years ago today, Layton was killed in a shoot-out with the police. On every anniversary of his death and at the exact time he died, he appears somewhere in the area. It's seven minutes after nine. That's when he died. I guess it was our turn tonight.

"He's gone!" shrieked one of Don's men. "He disappeared."

"Be careful when you leave," the waitress cautioned. "After he appears, someone in the area ends up dead."

Ghostly Matters and Suchlike
Discomfitures on Grand Canyon Road

Horribly embarrassing! That's what it was. It was horribly embarrassing to try and explain how I fell out of my 1931 Dodge Six Sedan on the entrance road of Grand Canyon National Park. To make matters worse the car, my pride and joy and now devoid of occupants, continued traveling down the road for exactly four and one third more miles.

That was the distance the insurance company determined the empty vehicle travelled before driving itself off the south rim of the Grand Canyon in a self-destructive plunge of eight hundred and fifty two feet. The insurance company also measured that distance.

Not a technical person, in my dark imaginings I

suspected disgruntled mechanical paraphernalia underneath the vehicle's hood concocted a vehicular suicide pact to avenge my not changing the oil or some other transgression. Of course, I hadn't planned on my car arriving at my destination several hours before me nor that in the seconds before its fatal dive it would make a scene driving right by horrified on-lookers enjoying afternoon   cocktails on the patio of the Bright Angel Lodge.

But I was to soon learn my suspicions were incorrect and the car's unsettling demise was not a suicide but the work of unearthly forces. After falling out of the car, as I lay there in the road watching it disappear I suddenly felt a sense of unease, as if I were being watched. Nervously, I got to my feet and looked around. Tall, dark green pine forests lined each side of the road. The trees did not stand close together but were loosely spaced approximately fifteen feet from each other. This allowed me to look into the forests seventy-five or so feet. Although I saw nothing, I thought I heard voices.

The sounds of the breeze blowing through the tall pines were like moans and whispers. Apparently the trees had taken note of my less than fortunate circumstances because I suddenly realized they were whispering about me.

"Did you see that guy fall out of his car? Did you ever see anything so dumb in your life Gerald?" I could tell from the conversation that the pine tree just off the dusty road and to my left was named Gerald. He knew I was watching him closely so he wisely chose not to answer that question posed by a catty female pine tree, which did not identify herself. For some reason, I thought her name might be Helen.

"Mister, you sure chose exactly the wrong time and place to fall out of your car," a voice from behind me said.

I spun round to find myself facing a three-foot tall turkey vulture or buzzard as some call them. I was getting fearful. It was one thing to encounter talking trees. I could rationalize that peculiarity by blaming the wind and an overactive imagination. But, a talking buzzard was more than my badly rattled nerves could handle.

"What kind of buzzard are you?" I replied, in nearly complete shock.

"I ain't a buzzard," was the indignant reply. "I'm a turkey vulture."

"Well, you go around eating dead animals." I don't think I'd be too particular about what I'm called," I said.

"I don't eat dead animals," he shot back. "I'm a

vegetarian."

"You're a vegetarian vulture?" I asked in amazement.

"Now I've seen it all," I thought.

"How is it you can talk?" I asked, in even greater amazement. It turned out to be a longer story than I wanted to hear.

"Fifty years ago on this exact date in 1883 I was riding shotgun on the Williams to Grand Canyon Stage Coach. There was only me and the driver, a mean hombre named "Nasty" Percival Montague. "Nasty" was not his given name, of course. There warn't no passengers, just Nasty Percival and me. We was haulin' mail and some packages but most important, we was carryin' four cases of whiskey. Me and Nasty Percival could absolutely not help ourselves and we opened a wooden case and each pulled out a bottle. We was drunk in no time."

Although I found the talking buzzard incredible and his story unbelievable, I stood and listened to him ramble on.

"It warn't too long before Nasty Percival and me got into a fight. He threw me off the stage as it was flying down the road and I landed just about where you did when you fell out of your velocipede (aka automobile). Without bothering to rein in the horses and stop, he jumped up on top the stage coach and screamed and cussed at me wavin' his bottle in one hand and his hat in the other, laughin' and carryin' on like Judgement Day was upon us."

"That still doesn't answer my question about how you can talk," I said.

"I'm gettin' to it, Mister," he said. "You're danged impatient."

"Sorry. It's just that I find your story captivating."

"Capti-what?" the vegetarian vulture said.

"Never mind," I replied. "Please get on with it."

"Anyway, as Nasty Percival screamed obscenities and laughed at me, something awful happened. I tried to warn him but he was too drunk and when I waved and yelled at him to duck down, he just got even more worked up and screamed and cussed at me even louder. That's when the coach went under the tree branch that knocked Nasty Percival's head clean off. It went bouncing into the ditch up the road about two hundred yards from here."

"Oh my lord," I said. Where did you bury the poor

man?"

"Well, that's the thing. The stagecoach kept rollin' and his body kept wavin', and curses were comin' out the collar of his shirt which is where he now poured his whiskey into. It was a awful sight. I run up the road to get his head for him but I got the gol darndest surprise instead. His head was layin' in the mud and facin' me see. And suddenly, the eyes opened wide and the head said, 'Where's Nasty?"

"That must have scared you mightily," I replied, still not accepting the outlandish reality of listening to a talking turkey vulture describe his conversation with the bodiless head of a drunken stagecoach driver.

"Oh, it did for sure, Mister. So I says to the head, I'll take you with me and we'll find Nasty."

"Oh no you won't,' the head says." 'I don't like Nasty so I'll just venture out on my own. I'm gonna' quit while I'm a head,' it says, tryin' to be funny."

"And then the head flew off in the opposite direction. That would be to the south," the turkey vulture said, looking down the road behind him.

"Anyways," the vulture continued, "I was left stranded here and somehow fell in with some Indians havin' a peyote party. You know, peyote is a drug that comes from the peyote cactus. Anyway, I was already drunk and once I got into the peyote, I don't remember nothin'."

"The next morning I woke up next to a very nice Indian lady with no teeth and seventeen kids. 'We're married,' she says. "But, I can't be married, I says. I already got me a wife. Well, as luck would have it, this was the mother of the tribe's medicine man. He got very upset with me and turned me into a turkey vulture which

I've been ever since. That's how I can talk. I used to be a human."

"What do you want with me?" I asked.

"I want you to adopt me and take me home. You can tell everyone I'm a new species of parrot."

"My friends will never believe that," I said. "They'll all know you're a vulture and they'll laugh at me."

"They'll believe you," the vulture said. "You don't look that smart yourself so your friends can't be that smart either. How about it? We got a deal?"

I took off running as fast as I could. I never ran four and one-third miles before, but I got to the Bright Angel Lodge just before last call for afternoon cocktails. It was late in October and the sun was already sinking low in the western sky. Darkness would soon be upon us.

As I sat there sipping my martini and listening to people tell me about the driverless car that rolled off the rim and fell into the canyon, I spied that turkey vulture standing on the roof of the lodge watching every move I made. A sense of deep apprehension was growing within me. For no good reason, my eyes wandered toward the window of my room. I was horrified to see a ghastly, phantom-like, disembodied head glaring back at me. I was praying the headless driver and his stagecoach and would not also arrive.

From behind me, someone suddenly put a hand on my right shoulder. A strong odor of horses and cheap whiskey filled the air. Trembling in horror, I dared not turn around.

A deathly, hollow voice turned my blood to ice when it exclaimed, "The stagecoach is here for you, Mister."

Oh, I never told you how I happened to fall out of my car. No, I surely didn't. But, that's another story.

The Ghost on Bright Angel Trail

"Help! Please help me!" she screamed. "Help! Oh, my god! No!" she shrieked, watching helplessly as a second boulder plummeted down the mountainside heading directly toward her.

Olivia Jousten heard only soft thuds when the first bulky rock tumbled down from above. There was no time to jump out of the path of the three hundred pound projectile, which broke both of her legs and pinned her firmly against the hard earth of the Bright Angel Trail.

It was late May in 1900 when history professor Dr. Edwin "Ed" Vespers began his hike down the Bright Angel on the south rim of the Grand Canyon. The abruptly descending trail made the walking difficult and less than a half mile into the hike his legs had become shaky. After covering nearly two miles, he was ready to turn around and re-trace his footsteps on the even more difficult climb out of the canyon. Then he heard cries for help coming from further down the trail behind a towering red cliff wall fifty feet ahead.

He quickly ran down the steeply sloping tan colored path to the massive red rock where the trail made a "switchback." There were countless of these one hundred and eighty degree turns on the ten mile long Bright Angel as the trail snaked back and forth across the south rim wall before eventually ending at the Colorado River. When he turned right on the switchback he immediately saw the reason for the calls for help. Seventy-five feet from where he stood was a woman lying on the trail, her body pinned by two rocks.

Ed ran down the trail, quickly reaching the spot where the woman lay. While the stones   were not huge, they were obviously weighty. Grasping the sharp edge of the reddish boulder resting on the woman's upper body, he pulled. But, it would not move. He pulled hard, and then again, using every bit of strength. The jagged rock was too heavy. It wouldn't budge. He had no better luck trying to move the second boulder. Ed could not produce even the slightest movement of either ponderous stone.

"Edwin, darling," she said. "You've come for me."

It was then he looked into her face. She was beautiful.

"I can't move the rock," he said. "I'll go for help."

"No, Edwin," she replied, grimacing in pain. "Just stay with me."

"Alright," he said, knowing the only help was on the canyon rim, a harsh two-mile climb of at least an hour.

He reached for her hand and held it in his. Although in great pain and obviously very weak, she was smiling. He was distressed and confused but forced himself to return her smile. Something powerful stirred within him. He must save her. Somehow, he must prevent her from dying. He must do something.

I will always love you, Edwin," she said. "Please remember that."

"But who are you?" he pleaded, in sudden, inexplicable grief. "I don't even know your name."

But her eyes had closed.

All Ed could do was cover her face and upper body

with his coat. Then he began his long, gloomy hike back up the Bright Angel Trail. When he reached the south rim nearly an hour later, his blistered feet and aching legs added to his physical exhaustion. But more troubling was his helplessness at being unable to do anything as he watched the woman die. And why did he feel such immense sorrow? He had never even seen her before their ill-fated meeting this day.

He walked toward the The Spires Hotel, wondering if the woman was also staying there. The twenty-room hotel was built four years earlier in 1896 at the terminus of the railroad line running from the south. As he walked up the front steps of the rustic wooden structure, guests seated at small, round tables on the front porch were enjoying their early afternoon cocktails. Ed walked through the lobby doors and went directly to   the registration desk.

"I'm Dr. Edwin Vespers and I want to report an accident on the trail," he said to the clerk. "A woman has died."

The clerk did not immediately reply but, with a stern expression, looked directly into Ed's eyes.

After what seemed like a prolonged silence, the clerk asked, "Where did this accident occur, Sir?"

"It was about two miles down the Bright Angel Trail. I can't give you a more accurate description than that."

Once again, the clerk stared at Ed with an intent and serious look on his face.

"Sir, would you please follow me into the office?" he finally replied, coming around the desk and gesturing toward the hallway behind him.

Ed followed the clerk into the small office behind the front desk. The clerk introduced him to the hotel manager, a man by the name of Manfred Mitchell.

"Sir, Dr. Vespers has an accident to report," he said, and then excused himself to return to his duties at the front desk.

"Ed noticed that as the manager shook Ed's hand, he studied him very carefully before he spoke. Ed wondered about the peculiar reactions of both the clerk and the manager. More importantly, he wanted to quickly get the young woman's unfortunate death reported and secure a badly need shot of whiskey. But, again he wondered, "Why did they both act so strangely?"

"Sir," the manager said, "the accident you are reporting was two miles down the Bright Angel near a switchback turning to the right, is that not correct?"

"Well yes, but how did you know? The clerk didn't tell you."

"There was no accident on the trail today, Sir," the manager replied.

"But," Ed began to reply, and was interrupted by the manager.

"Sir, the accident you saw did take place, but it occurred on this date exactly three years ago, May 19, 1897."

"What?" Are you mad?" Ed asked angrily. "I know what I saw."

"Please Sir," the manager responded. "Let me explain."

"I wish you would," Ed replied.

"Sir, the manager continued, "three years ago on this date a young woman named Olivia Jousten suffered the unfortunate accident which you apparently saw today. Your seeing her today is the third year she has appeared at that same unfortunate spot on the Bright Angel Trail. What you saw, sir, was a ghost."

"Nonsense," replied Ed. "You need to send someone down there immediately to bring the poor girl's body out of the canyon."

"Sir, the clerk has already sent someone down the trail to make sure there is no other injured hiker but, I will assure you, he will find nothing."

A puzzled and dejected Dr. Edwin Vespers left the manager's office and walked to the front porch to have his badly needed drink. As he sipped a whiskey, he suddenly remembered it was three years ago that he also visited the Grand Canyon. When he asked the waiter to check the dates of his prior stay with the front desk, the guest log showed he departed on May 18, the day before Olivia Jousten had died. "What would have happened had they met?" he wondered. "Or, had they actually spoken, if only for a moment? What would have happened if he stayed another day?" After an hour and three whiskies, he went back to his room and collapsed on his bed, physically and mentally exhausted. The alcohol helped him fall asleep quickly.

But sleep was fitful. When he slept, his sleep was sound, but he awoke from disturbing dreams of Olivia Jousten a half dozen times. In each of the dreams she walked into his room and put an envelope on the nightstand by his bed. The clarity and intensity of the dreams made them seem very real.

When he reached for her he felt her arm, her dress, and smelled her perfume. In his last dream, after Olivia laid the envelope on the bedside table, she turned toward him and smiling, leaned over and kissed him.

An annoying ray of bright sunlight shining through the opening between the two curtains on his east-facing window woke him up. His pajamas were soaked in sweat as was his bed. It had been a torturous night. As he sat staring toward the window, in the dim light of the early morning he saw an envelope on the small night table. He hesitated for a moment and then reached for it.

He stood up and walked to the window, pulling back the curtains to let in more sunlight. He could see clearly now. "Edwin" was beautifully written on the front of the envelope. Slipping his finger under the flap which was glued only at its tip, he reached inside and pulled out the card which read:

"Mr. and Mrs. William Jousten are proud to announce the wedding of their daughter Olivia to Dr. Edwin Vespers on Saturday, May 20, 1900."

Though Ed knew the date, he checked the calendar on the wall. Today's date was May 20, 1900.

Valle's Grudgeful Ghost

"It is hereby entered into the record that a statue honoring the notorious outlaw Kid Loco be erected in the town square," said the clerk. "The following justification of this expense is hereby noted below."

'The following factuals was put down by my hand on this Wednesday 19 August, 1897 at which time I swore under oath before Judge Delbert Flagg and City Concil that such goings-on occurred as below described and quotations was writ nearest my recollect. My signature hereby affixed. Jasper Bridwell, Administrator. (Judge F. assisting w/editing)"

Please don't hang me!" the man screamed. "You got the wrong man, I swear."

The crowd roared with laughter.

"This is a entertainin' hangin' aint it Lester?" one of the

spectators remarked.

Lester was laughing so hard he could barely reply and just shook his head meaning "Yeah."

"A man with a rope around his neck and sittin' on a horse don't have no credibility or options at that point, replied Judge Phlagg. Course, I can't blame you for tryin', Kid. You been runnin' wild as long as anyone can remember. But we got you dead to rights this time."

"I didn't do it, Judge. I swear," Kid Loco replied. "And I ain't Kid Loco neither."

The two denials got the crowd howling even more enthusiastically.

"Look kid, we been through all this," the Judge replied. You are the notorious Kid Loco and you gotta get hanged on account of the mischief you have propagated upon this community all these many years. Not to mention you're also a nuisance to the general public. Besides, it's about time we get you hanged so we can go over to the saloon to have a drink. It's 'Happy Hour' in a few minutes and you wouldn't want us to miss that now, would you?"

"Well no, course not Judge. But, how's about if I join you at the saloon and we discuss the situation?" Kid Loco pleaded.

"Sorry, Kid. We don't want to drink with no

condemned man. It's downright distasteful. You can understand that, I hope."

"Yes, I do Judge, Kid Loco replied. "But, I ain't Kid Loco. That's the truth."

The crowd bellowed with laughter once again, several of them rolling on the ground.

"Kid, we caught you sleepin' in the middle of a hundred head of cattle you rustled from Nester's ranch," the Judge said. "How much more guilty could you be?"

The man with the rope around his neck could see he wasn't about to convince anyone he hadn't rustled any cattle and he wasn't Kid Loco. He decided that his only hope was to admit that he actually was Kid Loco and appeal for mercy.

"Okay Judge, I'll admit to bein' Kid Loco. But, I am completely won over to your way of thinkin' about cattle rustlin'. It's a bad, bad thing. I was terrible misguided to be doin' it. I ain't ever gonna do it again, I swear."

The jovial crowd was snickering again, feeling fortunate they were able to attend such an amusing event. And it was free. "You'd have to pay fifty cents at the opera house in Flagstaff to see such amusement," one of the gawkers remarked.

"Kid, you promised you'd stop rustlin' a dozen times before."

"Well this time was different, Judge," Kid Loco said. "I was starvin' to death. A man's gotta eat don't he?"

"Yeah he does Kid. But, couldn't you have gone up to the kitchen at the ranch house and asked for a sandwich? If you was stealin' a hundred cows cause you was hungry, you musta had a powerful appetite."

The crowd was guffawing uncontrollably. This was surely the best hangin' they'd ever attended.

"Okay, so I accidentally took a hundred cows instead of one. I ain't ever gone to school to get educated so I ain't good with numbers. I woulda counted if I knew how and besides I didn't realize all them other cows tagged along."

The situation was this. No one had ever seen Kid Loco except when he was robbing them and in disguise. And he always used a different disguise when he perpetrated one of his crimes. Even worse, no one had ever seen Kid Loco out of disguise, leastwise not that they were aware. Therefore nobody actually knew what Kid Loco looked like in or out of disguise. Everyone who was robbed however did make a point of saying Kid Loco was always a very nice and courteous outlaw and never hurt nobody. Kid Loco's only fault was he enjoyed robbing people. "Nobody's perfect," they also said.

But the local newspaper, the Valle Expositor, commissioned an artist to draw a sketch of Kid Loco based on accounts from witnesses who had seen him in his various disguises. The artist asked the witnesses to imagine how Kid Loco would look if he wasn't in disguise. "Just give me your best guess how he might look," he told them. The artist made a composite sketch of the Kid from these guesses. Once the artist was done, all the eyewitnesses agreed this had to be Kid Loco, though no one ever claimed it to be a real scientific process.

George Bromley, a spitting image of the composite sketch of these eight peoples' imaginations, was travelling through Valle on horseback when he decided to stop and take a snooze under an inviting shade tree. When he woke up, he was surrounded by a hundred head of cattle and twenty men with rifles. Because of his uncanny resemblance to the artist's sketch, he was about to be lynched.

In truth, the cows had just wandered off. Even the real Kid Loco was innocent of any wrongdoing.

"Alright boys, give that horse a lick. We gotta' get this hangin' done cause we're late for 'Happy Hour.'"

"No, don't do that!" George Bromley aka Kid Loco yelled. "Hold on just a minute Judge. If you hang me you'll never know where I stashed all my loot."

"You mean you didn't spend it all on drinkin', gamblin' and women?" the judge replied.

"No Judge, I been real thrifty. I saved every penny I robbed and buried it all out there in the desert. If we can go over to the saloon and discuss this matter like genteel men I can direct you to my hidin' place."

"Sorry Kid," the judge said, "I don't believe you. Tell the good Lord we all said, "Hey."

"Why don't you tell me yourself, Judge Phlagg?" a voice suddenly boomed from above.

"Who said that?" asked Judge Phlagg?"

"It is me, the Lord Himself," the voice rumbled. "I come to chastise you for your grievous ways. You release this man now elsewise bad things are gonna happen real quick like."

The frightened crowd was immediately silent. The Lord was among them and he was not happy.

"Let him go, Judge!" someone screamed from the crowd. "Let him go!"

"Yeah Judge, we can't have the Lord mad at us," screamed another voice. "That just won't do."

"Let Kid Loco go," ordered the judge. "We're real sorry about this misunderstanding Lord."

"Well, I'll forgive you this time but you best take account of yourselves," the thunderous voice replied.

With that, George Bromley rode off, continuing his

journey north to the Grand Canyon to stage his "Amazing New York Ventriloquism and Voice Throwing Exposition."

"My best voice is the Lord," George laughed to himself. "I never thought it would save my life however."

The crowd was disappointed because no one got hanged but grateful because the Lord had spared them. But as they watched George Bromley ride away, a feeble voice from the rear of the group said, "I'm Kid Loco. I admit it before the Lord here and now. It's me what's been the mischief-maker for all these years. Please forgive me for my errant ways, Lord."

The astonished crowd looked toward the elderly man claiming to be Kid Loco.

"Aloysius Crackley?" an astonished Judge Phlagg gasped. "You're Kid Loco?"

"Fraid so," the ancient gentleman replied.

The on-lookers were shocked to learn Kid Loco was not only standing in their midst but was actually living amongst them. He was a very old man known by everyone in town. But their amazement abruptly became disbelief.

"How old are you, Aloysius?" asked Judge Phlagg.

"I'm ninety-seven years old, Judge," he replied.

The throng of people began snickering and then laughing loudly at Aloysius Crackley's claim that he was the notorious Kid Loco. "There was just no way this could be," they concluded.

"Well you have to understand that I got the moniker Kid Loco when I was much younger," Aloysius said.

That remark got the crowd to yukking hysterically once again. It was clear that not one person in the group believed Aloysius Crackley was Kid Loco.

"Aloysius, you're senile. Go on home before you embarrass yourself any further," said Judge Phlagg.

Aloysius was furious. "I worked danged hard to get my reputation of bein' a real nice and courteous outlaw so I could be a good example for others. I would write a few books about my sinful ways and how I reformed myself. That would fund my retirement, don't you know. Now you people don't believe I'm Kid Loco when the truth is staring you right in the face."

The laughter was deafening. The people had come to town to be entertained by a hanging but instead, they got their merriment by ridiculing Aloysius Crackley aka Kid Loco. Actually, their joyful yelps were also something of a stress reliever from the dizzying events that day. First there was the excitement of the scheduled hanging. Then they were scared out of their wits by a visit from the Lord, Himself. Then they were frustrated because the Lord told them to release the suspected Kid Loco. Then they were unhappy because nobody got hanged. And now, this little ninety-seven year old man claimed to be Kid Loco. But worst of all, they were a half an hour late for "Happy Hour." It had been a real bad day, save for the Lord's visit, of course. The crowd's laughter was sort of a soothing catharsis.

"You'll be sorry you didn't believe me," Aloysius screamed. "You denied me my hard earned reputation and ruined my retirement plans. You will pay the price for laughing at Kid Loco." Aloysius Crackley, aka Kid Loco, was a real unhappy man and that would prove to be a bad thing.

The laughter continued as the disgraced Kid Loco walked away from the crowd's ridicule.

Aloysius Crackley passed away that night. Only a couple of people attended the funeral a few days later. No one gave Aloysius Crackely, now known as the "Kid Loco Pretender, any further thought.

Oddly, however, once Aloysius Crackley died there were hardly any crimes being committed in northern Arizona. There were no more stagecoach or train robberies and no more bank robberies or cattle rustling. The Valle Expositor was about to close because there was no more news. "Maybe Aloysius Crackley really was Kid Loco," people began to think.

As if to underscore that suspicion, eerie things began to happen to those who laughed at Aloysius Crackley that fateful day of the planned hanging. The first ghastly occurrence was when Judge Phlagg woke up one morning with a rope around his neck. On his bedroom wall was scrawled, "I'll be back to finish you off, Judge. Regards, Kid Loco."

Then, when Merton Kingsley opened the door to his outhouse one night, he was horrified to see a ghostly Kid Loco holding a rope in his hand and pointing directly at him. "You're next!" the ghost screamed.

After those frightful incidents, no one went out of their house alone at night because Kid Loco haunted the town. And he ain't real nice and courteous no more. The ghost of Kid Loco was settling accounts.

Hopefully, erecting the earlier referenced statue of Kid Loco would appease him and stop the haunting.

It didn't.

Spirit Woman of the River

The brutal sun burned the land and anyone who foolishly chose to plod the ancient trails into the mystical inner canyon at mid-day. But only one man is hiking on this day as even the least experienced Grand Canyon trekker knows to find shade early and wait out the most intense heat in the hours before and after high noon. To lose the trail and run out of water in the hundred and twenty degree heat are fatal errors and bring a hard death.

Henry Tabor was that one man on the North Kaibab Trail on this day in late July, 1916. And he had lost the trail and was out of water.

The War to end all Wars raged in Europe and Henry, an Army sergeant, knew he would be leaving soon to join the fight against the Germans. He had long wanted to hike across the Grand Canyon and had no doubt in his mind he was up to the challenge. Although Henry had never before visited the desert country, he was in excellent physical condition and an experienced hiker. He figured he could make the hike in one day.

Before he began his hike, Henry prepared. He studied trail maps and carefully planned the hike and arrival times at different points along the way. An Ohio native, nearly all of Henry's hiking experience had been at lower elevations on level ground and moderate hills. His only concern was if the 7,000-foot altitude of the south rim would have any effect on him.

"The 23.6 mile hike across the Grand Canyon from the south to the north rim would be only a moderate challenge," Henry thought. "I'm in the best shape of my life and ready for anything."

That morning, he arrived at the Bright Angel Trailhead on the south rim before sunrise. He didn't even notice the higher altitude. The air was cool and he was ready to go. The hike to the Colorado River and the Canyon floor is 9.6 miles. As he started the hike, he remembered the floor of the Canyon was a vertical distance of 4,500 feet below the south rim. "It will be all downhill," he smiled to himself. "This will be a piece of cake."

Henry's pace was brisk and he quickly made the turns of the first few switchbacks. He estimated the grade of the trail to be about 10%, a fairly steep descent. It was twenty minutes later when Henry stood on a trailside rock to view the mile and a half rest house several switchbacks below his location.

"I've travelled nearly a mile," he estimated to himself, as he took a long drink of water. He knew he could re-fill the canteen at any of the rest houses along the 9.6-mile stretch to the Colorado River. After putting the cap on the canteen, he moved off the rock and back onto the trail. But now, something seemed wrong. His legs, which had been fine so far, now felt rubbery and seemed to wobble. It was the oddest feeling. It was as if both his legs would both collapse at any moment.

"Good Lord," he exclaimed to himself. "I've only come a mile and my legs are crumpling. How can that be? This is ridiculous."

Henry's over-worked legs were not prepared for the

continuously descending trail. His leg muscles were already badly stressed from "fighting" the steep downward slope of the trail with every step. He also had not drunk enough water since arriving in the extremely dry desert. He was dehydrated even before he began the hike. But he also wasn't drinking enough water as he walked and the dehydration was worsening.

When he arrived at the mile and a half house he decided to rest. He stretched out on the ground and rested his head on the light backpack. It seemed like only minutes since he pulled his cap over his eyes to block the sun when he heard voices.

"Who is on the trail this early?" he wondered.

But when he looked at his watch, it was just after nine-thirty. Two other hikers waved as they walked past him.

"Good lord, I must have slept two hours."

The sun was high now and the day was beginning to warm. It reminded him the floor of the canyon is a much lower altitude than the canyon rims. Because of this, it is a desert environment with temperatures routinely soaring to over one hundred degrees. But, he was confident the heat would not be a problem. He decided to calculate how far he was behind his carefully planned schedule.

"Figuring a minimum of three miles of hiking per hour

and losing at least two and a half hours, I'm seven to eight miles behind my schedule," he said to himself.

Henry definitely felt better after stopping to rest but it had taken time. He realized he had to quickly hike to the Canyon floor, cross the Colorado River, and begin his fourteen-mile trip to the North Rim on the North Kaibab Trail. He planned to hike all day and reach the North Rim before dark. It was a bad decision. The Colorado River was still eight miles away.

"If I move quickly, I can reach the river by noon," he promised himself, as he again started down the Bright Angel Trail.

An hour later and four and a half miles into his hike, Henry reached Indian Gardens. The numerous cottonwood trees were a tempting shelter from the hot sun but he was intent on reaching the North Rim before dark. It was still another five miles of rugged hiking to the Colorado River.

He never thought about the sun being a serious problem. But it took him over two hours to reach the river because the temperature had risen to ninety-six degrees and he was forced to stop several times to rest in the shade. As he watched the massive Colorado's coffee colored water rushing past, he was not feeling well. He wondered if the sun was affecting him.

It cost fifty cents to ride across the river in the canvas boat. When the boat docked at the north shore, Henry quickly got back to his hike. He was now walking north along Bright Angel Creek on the North Kaibab Trail. He passed by Bright Angel Campground and was soon entering the "inner gorge" of Bright Angel Canyon, the most dangerous section of the hike. For over seven miles, the trail runs through the 1.7 billion year old black rock of the Vishnu Schist and the Great Unconformity.

The temperature had now risen to one hundred and thirteen degrees. Henry, already dehydrated and exhausted, quickly became disoriented and wandered off the main trail onto an animal path leading into the brush. The black rock of the canyon walls made the temperature even hotter. Henry pushed on but was struggling badly. When he removed the cap of the one-gallon canteen, the flask slipped from his hands and rolled down the narrow path spilling precious water along the way. He rushed to retrieve the canteen but stumbled and fell face first onto the ground. He raised his head from where he lay and saw the water still spewing from the canteen resting mouth down against a rock six feet from him.

"My god, I can't get up," he gasped, as he tried to stand but could not. "I'm burning up," he muttered, and noticed his pulse was racing. He was dizzy and confused. "I should be sweating but my skin is dry," he thought.

He remembered reading a note on heat stroke but was too groggy to remember what it said. His eyes closed as the sun blistered his tortured body.

When his eyes finally opened, it was dark and cool. He felt weak but much better than he remembered feeling before he became unconscious. But he was not on the trail. He was in a bed on the ground inside some kind of shelter. Although still a bit shaky, he rolled to his left side and propped himself up on his elbow. He must have spent the night there and the soft light of early morning now shone outside the little building.

"Is anyone there?" he called. "Hello! Is anyone there?"

A small Indian woman about four and a half feet tall appeared in the doorway of the shelter. She walked over to him and handed him a leather flask. She motioned for him to drink.

It was water and it tasted good, much better than any he had ever tasted.

"Come with me," she told him. "You are better now."

That he was able to stand surprised him.

"Follow," she said.

He walked behind the small woman along a trail, though he didn't know which one. The trail ran very straight and sloped downward. In minutes, they arrived at the Colorado River.

"You are safe now," she smiled, and she pointed eastward indicating he should follow the river.

He walked a few steps along the riverbank and turned to thank her. But she was gone.

Then he heard the faint but gruff voice of the boatman who had ferried him across the river in the canvas boat. Walking further up the river toward the sound, he saw the canvas boat tied up near some bushes at the water's edge. The boatman was unloading two hikers and their gear from the small craft.

As the two men talked, it became clear that three days had passed since Henry began his hike. Henry described his close brush with death and the small Indian woman who saved his life.

"Once she led me to the river, she vanished," Henry said.

"You aren't the first person to tell me about her," the boatman replied. "There have been many others whose lives she has also saved."

"But who is she?" Henry asked.

"There is an Indian legend that tells of an Anasazi woman who was careless and lost her little daughter in the inner canyon over a thousand years ago. The legend says the child went missing and was later found, but it was too late. The young girl had died from exposure to the hot sun."

"That's a sad story," Henry replied.

"It's very sad," replied the boatman. "The legend also says that because the careless woman lost her daughter, she must wander through the canyon forever and find those who are lost and help them find their way to safety. She always brings them to the river."

"So she saves all the people who get lost?" Henry asked.

"No, she cannot find everyone," the boatman replied. "When someone dies in the canyon, she once again suffers just as she did when she lost her daughter. At night, people often hear a woman crying. Some say it is the strong breeze blowing through the trees. But those of us who live here know it is the spirit woman of the river."

Cottonwood Liar's Club

The chilling hand of death grasped him the moment he walked through the front door of his home. Death, the morbid partner of the living, enveloped the house and bore down upon him like a cumbrous shroud. It tweaked his every sense, as if to intimidate and remind him that all was not right on this night. The door's handle had been icy to the touch and the sour smell of the dead permeated the house.

Only minutes earlier he was spinning a tall tale at the Ugly Dog Saloon. What he expected to be an uneventful evening had turned into a nightmare. It was April 2, 1930, the first Wednesday of the month, the night of the regularly scheduled meetings of the Cottonwood Liar's Club.

Therein were several lies right off the bat. First,

75

nobody in the group was actually a liar, at least not in the dishonorable sense. They were all upstanding, forthright citizens. Secondly, they didn't really have a club, rather a group of seventeen Cottonwood citizens who got together once a month to see who could tell the biggest tall tale.

Each meeting the group would choose a monthly winner for the best yarn. The winner would then receive a five-dollar bill. At each meeting, five members would take their turn competing in the story telling. This night was Freddy Slater's turn. He and four other club members competed with their version of a great whopper.

Haney was also on tonight and he always had a great story. In fact, Haney won the competition six different months in 1929. A couple of club members dropped out last year because they just couldn't compete with the daunting Haney. Then there was Lander Berkfield. Lander owned a ranch east of town. He was in World War One and had a lot of true experiences, which he could embellish. The other two boys, Oscar Jenkins and Willy Totz, were new to the club and hadn't quite gotten the hang of concocting a good tall tale. But, Freddy wasn't worried about anyone tonight. He was confident he would win because he had a real whopper to share.

The meeting was always held at "The Ugly Dog," thought by some to be the best saloon on Center Street. That there were only two other taverns on Center Street didn't make its informal "best saloon" rating any less of an honor however.

At exactly seven o'clock that evening, the competition began. There was always a crowd of onlookers who came to hear the wild stories and drink beer. There were at least one hundred people in the room. It was a guaranteed to be a rollicking good time.

Willy Totz went first. He was nervous, hesitant and stumbled over words, quickly losing the crowd. It was too bad because he actually had a pretty good recital about Chinese pirates visiting America before Columbus and a Chinese junk loaded with gold buried on the banks of the Verde River.

Then Oscar Jenkins got up to try his luck. He had a real boring chronicle of a ghostly   wagon train that plodded through town once a year when there was a full moon and some accompanying cosmic oddity. It didn't make a lot of sense and besides, he was pretty drunk when he started talking and polished off several more beers before he sat down. He got bad marks in story delivery and for general poor content.

As usual, Lander Berkfield did a good job. He gave a

narrative of a World War One battle in some remote town in Belgium occupied by zombies and other disgruntled creatures, which walked around making noises at night. All told, he did a pretty good job but the idea of zombies didn't catch on too well with the crowd that particular night.

Haney's presentation was next. He spun a great tale about a very unhappy woman who stole the weather. She could return pieces of the weather at her own discretion. If she was unhappy, which of course she often was, she could return storms. If she wanted people to suffer, she could return sunny and very hot. She could make it snow in July if she chose. It may not sound like it makes a lot of sense written down as it is, but his presentation was powerful and credible. Freddy Slater would have a hard time beating Haney but he still thought he could.

Finally, it was his turn and he began his story. "Everyone knows that Tuzigoot National Monument and its ancient Sinagua ruins are located in the town of Clarkdale which is very near where we are gathered tonight. What you don't know however is that eight months ago there was a very mysterious discovery over on Cleopatra Hill just above Clarkdale. For those of you from out of town, Clarkdale and the Tuzigoot Ruins are set hard against the base of Cleopatra Hill while the town of Jerome sits at its summit.

What archaeologists discovered was a large, reddish rock nearly ten feet high with many petroglyphs drawn on it. This rock was sitting at the side of a trail and thousands of people had passed by it over the years but never even noticed it. This was probably   because it sat among several other similar rocks and was not particularly conspicuous and also because the side with the petroglyphs faced away from the trail.

You might ask what makes this particular rock so mysterious. First, the petroglyphs on this rock are unlike any rock art in the area. Second, these petroglyphs are very old, pre-dating other rock art by at least seven thousand years. While drawings of supernatural beings and visions are not uncommon in this part of the country, the drawings on this rock are very unusual in that they are solid, black spectral forms with red eyes. The drawings of these spirits are very frightening because the red eyes are set in yellow scleras, and they seem to follow a person as one moves from right to left and back again. These petroglyphs and this particular spot on Cleopatra Hill emphasize the unholy and death. The place was obviously considered a place of exceptional evil.

At first the archaeologists thought the large rock was a tombstone, yet no body was found when the excavation team dug into the ground beneath it. Instead, they found a clay tablet with some kind of symbols or writing on it. However, the Indians who lived in this area in ancient times had no written language. So the archaeologists had to figure out whether the symbols were actually writing and, if so, determine what the writing said. It took many months of study and consultation with archaeologists in other countries before they finally deciphered it.

They concluded some ancient people carefully buried the clay tablet under the rock because it contained some kind of evil curse. By burying the tablet, they could ward off the curse. However, there was no further trace of these ancient people after they buried the clay tablet with its evil curse.

Apparently, burying the clay tablet with the evil curse didn't work," Freddy joked, "because the entire population disappeared." The audience laughed.

"What I am now going to read to you has never been made public. It was only with great persistence and the intervention of a considerable quantity of Tennessee Whiskey that my friend at the Archaeological Museum in Flagstaff availed me the opportunity to copy the precise interpretation locked in their files.

At this point I must ask the ladies and any children present (there were none) to leave the room. What I shall tell you next is the most heinous and dreadful of curses and not fit for genteel ears."

Although there were only five women present, they unanimously objected and insisted on staying to hear the rest of the story. Freddy continued.

"Alright then ladies, you were warned. Here is what was inscribed on the tablet.

'What is written here is a call to the hideous creatures of the underworld, those ghastly   evil spirits of the night who destroy men and gods, casting them into eternal damnation.'

Arise O Lorgun! Come from the hellish depths of the Underworld and carry out my demonic bidding. Gather all of those around me and send them plummeting into your unblest sanctum, holding their souls for all eternity."

The room was suddenly plunged into darkness and desperate screams pierced the walls of the saloon and were heard in the street. Freddy Slater fell backward onto the floor, momentarily stunned. Then there was a deathly silence.

In a few moments two policemen arrived and entered The Ugly Dog Saloon. One of them replaced a fuse and the lights abruptly came back on. As Freddy sat on the floor next to the bar, he suddenly realized he and the two policemen were the only ones in the saloon. Everyone else had vanished. At first he thought he might have been knocked unconscious but he quickly realized that wasn't the case. Where were the other hundred plus people who had been sitting at the tables listening to him tell his story just moments before?

The policemen asked the same question but Freddy had no answer. As he looked around the barroom, everything appeared to be in order. Nothing had been disturbed and partially consumed drinks and dinners sat on the tables. Everything was in order except there were no people where over one hundred had been sitting and standing moments earlier. Freddy described to the policemen everything that happened and even gave them a copy of his story.

"Did you put this curse on these people?" one of them asked.

"Of course not," Freddy replied.

"This looks like a curse to me," said the other policeman.

"We were having our monthly meeting of the Cottonwood Liars Club. My entire story is made up. None of it is true. We never tell true stories at the Liars Club. All the stories are tall tales, things we invent ourselves."

Freddy walked home, shaking his head in disbelief. "What happened that night? Where did all the people go?"

He arrived at his house and walked through the front door into his living room. Although no lights were lit, an eerie bluish glow afforded dim illumination of the parlor. With his body shaking and cold sweat beading on his face, he cautiously crept toward the mysterious faint light.

As he reached the entrance to the room, a raspy, unearthly voice sounded from the grim shadows, "You summoned me and I have come."

It was then that Freddy saw the hideous creature, which was exactly as he described in his story. It was a shadowy, black, spectral-like being hovering above the floor. The apparition's head and indistinct neck descended onto wider shoulders, and featureless straight arms pressed against a solid body, which tapered downward with its lower extremity fading into an indistinct mist. The creature's glowing red eyes set in bright yellow scleras peered directly into Freddy's soul.

"I did not summon you!" Freddy screamed in utter terror. "The curse in my story was a lie, something I made up."

"Freddy, who are you yelling at?" exclaimed a familiar voice behind him.

Freddy spun around to face his wife his wife Meredith.

"Don't you see it, Meredith?" he shrieked.

"See what, Freddy?" Meredith replied, in a tone of noticeable anxiety.

"The creature, Meredith!" Freddy screeched, as the deathly shadow moved toward him.

"Freddy, calm down, please. There is no creature. What are you talking about?"

"Meredith, it's right in front of me," Freddy wailed.

"Freddy!" Meredith replied firmly, "you're scaring me. Stop this insanity now! There's nothing there."

Then it was Meredith who suddenly gasped in horror. There was nothing there, including Freddy.

A Bush in Flagstaff

Oklahoma blew away. So did Kansas. A bunch of other states in the Midwest blew away too. My farm, which was eleven miles north of Tulsa and just outside of Sperry, blew away just like my neighbors' farms. In 1931 we didn't know about crop rotation or erosion prevention. A bad drought dried up the topsoil and the wind churned it into monumental dust storms. Huge dark clouds of dust blackened the skies over New York and Washington as millions of acres of prime farmland blew east and into the Atlantic Ocean.

Like everybody else, I left my ruined farm to go west. The bank took my car but the Baptist minister sold me his old Ford sedan for four dollars. It needed a clutch and tires and he didn't have the money to get it fixed. I didn't have the money either but an Indian friend of mine over at Skiatook cobbled a repair on the clutch and scrounged four tires about seventy percent used up. With $67.31 cents in my pocket, I drove eleven miles down to Tulsa and got on Highway 66 and headed west.

In five days I reached Arizona. It was slow going because of the blowing dust and long stretches of Route 66 weren't paved. Some of the road was made out of wood planks. Often, the road wasn't wide enough to let two cars pass so each one had to slow down and drive half on and half off the road, being careful to not let the tires off the road sink into the dust.

Although food was cheap, gas was expensive at fifteen cents a gallon. When I stopped in Flagstaff late that night I slept in my car as I couldn't afford a hotel. The clutch on the Ford was slipping and a local garage told me they would charge $1.47 to adjust it. Flagstaff was a real nice town so I decided to look around while they worked on my car. That's when I saw the Hotel Weatherford. It was beautiful and majestic. An outside balcony on the second floor overlooked the street and the surrounding buildings. "Wish I had the money to stay there," I fantasized.

I walked inside to take a look. Across the lobby to my left, two French doors opened to a restaurant. There was also a small nook with a couch and table where people might enjoy a cocktail and look out on the street. At the back of the lobby there was a phone booth underneath the staircase, which led to the second floor. Straight down the hallway was the main bar. "I'll only be here one time," I thought to myself. "I'll splurge and have a beer."

The bar was just as impressive as the hotel. Sturdy, dark wood pillars supported a massive canopy over three alcoves, with a huge mirror built into the center and largest of them. Tall stacks of beer glasses lined up like soldiers in formation stood in front of the mirror. I suppose I didn't look particularly prosperous because the bartender only charged me five cents for a beer.

He was a real nice guy and like most bartenders, he was talkative. For some reason, the conversation got around to ghosts. "You know, this place is haunted," he confided to me.

"I'm afraid I don't believe in that sort of thing," I replied.

"You would if you saw what I've seen," he countered. "She's in the ballroom. People see her there all the time.

They've seen her up on the second floor too."

We talked for a while longer and I finished my beer.

"I still don't believe in ghosts," I laughed, as I got up to leave. "It's been nice talking to you though. Be careful of those ghosts," I chided him.

I walked over to the garage to get my car and once again was heading west on Route 66. I found myself behind a large, slow moving tank truck hauling a load of gasoline. Moving at a snail's pace, I impatiently followed the truck knowing it was impossible to pass on the narrow road.

As I was approaching the city limits of Flagstaff there was a small rock outcropping in a meadow to my right. It was a spit of stone and dirt about fifty feet in length and sat five feet off the ground. Sitting on the very end of this rather unremarkable but scenic projection was a small green bush about two feet high. I don't know what kind of bush it was, but there were others like it around the meadow as well a large number of tall green pine trees characteristic of the Flagstaff area. But this bush sat alone at the end of the miniature cliff, like it was threatening to jump off at any moment.

But then the strangest thing happened. In my entire life, nothing like this ever happened before nor has it since.

The large gasoline tank truck had stopped to wait for traffic to clear. As I sat behind the truck, I stared at the small rock promontory and the lone bush sitting at its edge. For some reason, I felt compelled to pull my car off the road and walk over and take a closer look at this very pleasant setting. It was a scene that even an average artist could easily turn into a beautiful painting.

"No, I have a long way to go so I better keep moving," I thought. "I don't have time for sightseeing."

But something was pulling me toward the bush and its beautiful surroundings. "This is ridiculous," I told myself. "I really have get on my way."

Just the same, I found myself turning the steering wheel to my right and slowly driving the car to the side of the road. I was shaking my head in wonderment of my bizarre compulsion to stop and look at a rock and a bush. "Maybe it was the altitude getting to me," I thought. It's sixty-five hundred feet high in this area, the highest point on Route 66. "Besides, we conservative farmers just don't do irrational things like stop the car and look at a bush," I laughed to myself.

However, I found myself so strongly drawn toward the bush that I was walking quickly, almost running to it. When I reached the small rock plateau, I stepped upward on four small boulders and walked across its top and over to the bush. I sat down on a small rock and stared at the bush for the longest time. The bush was sage green in color with fifteen or twenty small branches. It was barely above my knee in height and was rather ordinary looking with nothing exceptional about it.

Of course the minute I got out of my car, the traffic started moving again. As I looked over toward the road I could see cars were travelling along pretty quickly now. It was a beautiful day with the sun shining, although a bit cool as might be expected at this altitude. There wasn't a cloud in the sky and it was a perfect day for driving. But, I found it impossible to pull myself away from the bush.

I knew I was wasting time but I continued to sit there looking at the solitary shrub, completely unable to leave the rock on which I sat and get back to the business of driving to California. The bush had a hold on me in a way I cannot explain. I guess fifteen minutes had gone by when something happened that, even to this day twenty-six years later, I cannot explain.

As I gazed at the bush it began to shimmer, much like heat rising from a concrete road. Then it began to alternately glimmer and become wavy. Even in the sunlight the bush glowed brightly but suddenly, the hazy but radiant apparition of a young woman appeared before me. Clothed in a long white dress, she was pale, blond, and beautiful. To say I was astonished would be an understatement.

She looked directly into my eyes and smiled. "You don't believe in ghosts and the supernatural," she said softly. "Maybe you will change your mind some day."

"Maybe I will," I stuttered, "thoroughly amazed at what I was witnessing and perplexed at being unable to find words to say to her.

I heard thunder in the distance, two or three rolling, muffled booms. I glanced at the sky. It was bright blue and no clouds whatsoever.

"Are you expecting rain?" she teased.

"No, not at all," I replied, with some embarrassment.

"I wouldn't think so, either" she added, gently smiling.

Still bewildered I couldn't speak.

"You should go now," she said. "It's safe."

She disappeared as quickly as she had come, leaving me sitting on the rock and staring at the sage colored bush. I got up and walked back to the car, astounded by my encounter.

As I pulled onto the road and looked into the distance, I saw enormous clouds of black smoke billowing over the hilltops about four miles away. There must have been a bad accident, no doubt the source of the rumbling I mistook for thunder.

A few minutes later I encountered a long line of stopped cars. The road ahead was blocked. A gasoline tanker had exploded and killed fourteen people in cars following behind the truck. It was over four hours before the road was opened again.

I drove by the charred hulks of the gasoline tanker and the cars in back of it, knowing that if I hadn't stopped at the bush, I would have been behind the truck when it exploded. I too would have been killed.

Crazy Hal of Tuba City

"They laughed every time they saw him. They couldn't help themselves," Charlene Otero told me.

Charlene was 87 years old and lived over near Dinnebito just off Indian Highway 41. The agency sent me to check on her every few weeks to make sure she was doing okay.

"Nobody believed Hal was really an Indian," Charlene continued. "But he always insisted that he was. At first, I didn't believe him either. His real name was Harold Malinowski and he was from Pittsburgh. He had blond hair and blue eyes and was very tall at six feet two inches. He didn't look anything like an Indian is supposed to look and not many Indians are born in Pittsburgh and have blond hair and blue eyes."

"Please, tell me more," I asked.

"Hal came to Tuba City in 1917. I was a young girl then, only seventeen, and I lived in town. For some reason, I was fascinated with Hal. Even though he was forty-two, and much older than me, we became good friends. I thought that since he was forty-two he was a very old man.

The reason people laughed at Hal was because he would always go out to the dinosaur tracks about six miles southwest of Tuba City. You've seen the ancient tracks, which are "frozen in stone." Hal would sit on the rocks and stare at those dinosaur tracks for hours. Everybody said he was waiting for a herd of dinosaurs to walk by.

I began going out to the dinosaur tracks with Hal and he would tell me stories about the dinosaurs and a very ancient tribe called the Onotwah. Hal said all the land around Tuba City is a land of spirits and ghosts. The dinosaurs died here but their spirits live. You can only see them at certain times.

It was the same with the Onotwah. They are here but can only be seen at certain times. He was waiting to see the Onotwah because the tribe had a large village near the dinosaur tracks many years ago. 'The village is there now,' Hal said. 'But we cannot see it. We can only feel the presence of the ancient ghosts.'

However, when I went to the library to research the Onotwah I found there was no such tribe. I asked him why that was. He just smiled and said, 'You shall see, Charlene. You shall see.'

But then something bad happened," Charlene continued. "World War One was raging and Hal had been in the Army. Hal ran away from the Army because he had a vision that he was a reincarnated Onotwah warrior and his people needed him. The Army's Military Police were searching for him and they came to Tuba City to arrest him because he was a deserter."

"Did they arrest him?" I asked.

"Hal told me he needed to be at the dinosaur tracks just one more day," she replied, side-stepping the answer to my question. 'Please Charlene,' he pleaded. 'Help me hide from them for just one more day.'

"But Hal," I told him. "You are a deserter. You are a coward who won't fight for our country."

'No, Charlene,' he replied. 'It is true I left the Army but I am not a coward. I am a great warrior of the Onotwah Tribe. I have fought many battles. I am not of this country or this time. I lived many years before the country known as the United States was born. I must go back to my people because they too face great danger. I must protect them or they will die.'

"No offense, Charlene," I said, "but it sounds to me like Hal was telling you 'tall tales."

"No," Charlene replied, as she looked through the window of the room and toward the far mesa. "He was telling me the truth but I was young and didn't understand."

It was then I noticed tears slowly rolling down her cheeks. "Why are you crying, Charlene?"

"If I tell you why, you will laugh at me, just like they laughed at Hal so many years ago."

"I promise I won't laugh," I said. "I promise."

"Then would you promise me something else?" she asked.

"Yes," I said, completely fascinated by her story.

"You must take me to the dinosaur tracks today by two pm. Will you do that for me?"

"Charlene," I replied, the dinosaur tracks are over fifty miles from here. There are other people I must see today."

"Please," Charlene replied. Do this one thing for me. I have never asked you for anything before. Besides, if you don't take me to the dinosaur tracks, I won't tell you the rest of the story," she smiled.

She was so charming I couldn't turn her down. "Alright," I told her. "I will have to take a day off work to do it. Now, tell me the rest of the story. We must leave soon if we are to be at the dinosaur tracks by two PM." I didn't understand why we needed to be there at a certain time as the tracks had been there many millions of years but, she was old and I humored her.

"I hid Hal in my house that night. The next morning we got up before dawn and Hal drove us out to the dinosaur tracks in his old Chevrolet coupe. But something unbelievable happened."

"What was that?" I asked.

"When we got to the dinosaur site, instead of just the flat rock ridge there was a huge village with thousands of people. The village was bigger than Tuba City.

Hal was smiling. 'My time has come,' he said. 'Remember when you asked me about the Onotwah tribe, Charlene? I said, you shall see.' As Hal walked toward the village he changed into a much younger man with long black hair and brown eyes. 'Come with me, Charlene,' he called to me. 'Be my wife.'

"But I didn't go. What happened was so overwhelming, I was afraid and confused."

We then left her small home and drove towards Tuba City and the dinosaur tracks site. We talked as I drove and it became very clear to me that Hal was the love of Charlene's life. The time passed quickly as her stories were so interesting, and it seemed like only minutes had   passed when we arrived. I pulled my truck off the main highway and onto the dirt road. It was nearly two PM.

Charlene was facing me as I helped her out of the truck.

Although her face was tired and wrinkled, her eyes suddenly opened wide and her face broke into a broad smile. I thought she was smiling at me and I smiled back.

But then I noticed Charlene's eyes were looking toward something behind me. I turned around to see what she was looking at and I was astonished. It was just as Charlene had described when Hal walked away from her on this same rock plateau so many years ago.

"Thank you," she said, as she walked toward a huge village of thousands of people not there a moment before.

Less than fifty feet from where we stood, a handsome, smiling warrior was waving at her. As Charlene's aged body hobbled toward the village, she became straighter and walked ever faster, her hair becoming coal black. By the time she reached the very happy man, she had turned into a much younger woman.

They embraced and kissed, and walked hand in hand into the village. Charlene was smiling happily when she turned to me and waved. I waved back.

They walked a few steps further and the village slowly faded leaving nothing but the desert.

And the ancient dinosaur tracks.

Ghost Horse of Kayenta

"In truth, I have not seen him. But some of the old people tell of the Ghost Horse. Charlie Big Hawk over at Many Farms saw him back in 1903 near Carson Mesa northwest of his house. And Billy Gonzalez from Tes Nez Iah says his grandfather saw him once over by Meridian Butte. The Ghost Horse is the combined spirit of the great warriors and brave horses of ancient times. You can see him in the rock art.

The horses were not here before the Spaniards came. History tells us the conquistadores brought the horses to our land. But that is the white man's history. The rock art is Indian history. It tells us the white man's history is wrong. The horse was here long before men ever came to our sacred land. Oh yes, horses were here in ancient times before man came into this world. They were here fifteen million years ago in what the white man calls the Late Miocene period.

We Indians refer to the time before man as the 'time of the gods.' These ancient horses were called Merychippus and were the father and mother of all the other horses. They were six feet tall and weighed one thousand pounds. But long ago, Merychippus went away. They went away just as our people went away when they left their cliff houses and other dwellings, which are all around us even now. The ancient horses and our ancestors left this land at very different times but they left for the same reason. The evil ones came from the north.

Although Merychippus would die like all other living things, his spirit remained and is with us today. It is the same for the ancient people, our ancestors. They also died but their spirits remains with us today.

Originally, our people also came from the north. The evil ones made us leave. The evil ones are not mortal men. They are ghosts and spirits that bring misfortune, sickness and death. Long ago the Sky God condemned them to prowl the Earth and witness the happiness of those who live as mortals. The Sky God makes them see the happiness they lost because of their evil deeds. But they also bring misfortune, sickness and death.

The Ghost Horse does not come here often but   when he does, there is always a reason. The Ghost Horse takes two forms, pitch black or pure white. If he is black when he comes, it means evil is present and the ghosts of the north are here. He will help our people fight them.

But if he is white, all is well and everyone is safe. He comes to reassure us and remind us that his spirit is always with us and he has come to help us."

Ahiga Nogana lay in his hospital bed listening to his grandfather Joseph Rameriz tell of the Ghost Horse.

"Will the Ghost Horse help me, Grandfather?" he asked.

"Yes, Ahiga, he will help you. He will come and make you well."

"Father," Miriam said firmly, "why do you fill his head with nonsense? The Ghost Horse is a myth. Do not tell my child he will see the Ghost Horse. He will just be unhappy when the Ghost Horse never appears."

"It is alright, Mother," Ahiga said. "I know I am going to die. I am not afraid. But, I believe the Ghost Horse will come and I will see him."

"You see, Father," Miriam scolded Grandfather Joseph, "you see what you have done. He is hoping for something that will never happen."

With that, Miriam turned and left the room. Grandfather Joseph smiled at Ahiga.

"The young people have forgotten our beliefs, Ahiga. When you grow up, you must never forget what I have taught you. Everyone today is too busy to remember the important things. Please do not become one of those forgetful people."

"I won't, Grandfather," Ahiga said softly. "Grandfather, I don't feel so good. I heard the doctor tell Mother I would die very soon. I think it is time."

"No, Ahiga," Grandfather Joseph said, as tears began to roll on his cheeks. "Do not leave me, Ahiga. You must not die, Grandson."

The doctor and Mother walked into the room. The doctor looked very serious and Mother was crying. Ahiga knew it was his time. The doctor nodded at Grandfather.

Grandfather Joseph smiled softly as he looked toward Ahiga. But Ahiga was grinning broadly and looking out the window. He suddenly began to laugh as he pointed toward the sky.

There was only one bright cloud in the clear blue sky. It was the shining image of a great white horse triumphantly rearing up on his hind legs. Ahiga and Grandfather were both laughing. Ahiga would live.

The Ghost Horse had come.

"Night Sky in Williams"

"It's a Royston! This is unbelievable!" I exclaimed under my breath. But, I wanted to shout it out loud. Trying to contain myself, I glanced toward the bartender, wondering if he had noticed the shock which must certainly have registered on my face when I recognized the artist who created the painting in the scratched, chipped gold frame. This beautiful piece of art by the famous artist Thomas Royston was displayed on the wall just a few feet from where I sat. As I was an art critic, there was no doubt in my mind this was an authentic work by that well known genius.

Although I was not familiar with that particular painting, "Night Sky in Williams," Royston's unique stylistic method was readily identifiable. Any Royston painting was easily worth two million dollars. And it was just hanging there, waiting for some drunk to throw beer on it or deface it in some other way. "They can't possibly know what they have here," I groused to myself. "They are standing here "pulling pints" as they say in England, and that Royston is worth more than the hotel, maybe all the hotels in Williams, Arizona."

It was 1947 and I stopped overnight en route to a vacation at the Grand Canyon. As I drove through Williams, I saw the Hotel Ammerman. It was a beautiful and inviting place so I stopped and went into the lobby. The staff was friendly and the atmosphere luxurious. The prices were not bad, actually quite cheap. I had checked in an hour earlier and was now enjoying a Manhattan in the hotel's exquisite Chief Wise Eagle Saloon.

The first Manhattan had gone down smoothly and I was getting ready to order a second. I was also pondering if I might buy the painting from the hotel and then re-sell it at a very nice profit.

"Yes, please!" I chirped to the bartender. "Another Manhattan, my good man," I replied, when he asked if I would like another drink. I didn't normally talk like that so my first Manhattan must have been a fairly strong potation. Then I began thinking about Thomas Royston. What an incredible artist he was.

Royston was at the forefront, if not the originator, of

the Urban Reality Movement. This particular school became popular on the art scene in the early 1920's. It portrayed stark, harsh images of urban blight despoiling nature. Homely buildings, ugly automobiles and factory waste portrayed against dying trees and flowers emphasized the ravages man wrought upon the Earth. The works of that movement, although somewhat depressing, were intricately constructed, precisely detailed, and passionately targeted for maximum impact. Royston was the leading artist at that time and his paintings were bringing incredible money.

Royston was also a mysterious loner who would disappear for months at a time then suddenly turn up someplace far from his New York base. In 1928, at the very height of his popularity, he vanished once again. At first, no one thought much about it. However, several months went by and then several more months passed. In all, seven months elapsed and there was still no sign of Royston.

In early 1929, Royston's body was discovered in Williams, Arizona. He had been shot three times. His murderer was never found. Royston's premature death caused his paintings to skyrocket in price. Everyone, it seemed, had to have a Royston. The limited number of his works also helped their value increase tremendously. Frankly, I thought I was familiar with every one of Royston's major works but I had never come across "Night Sky in Williams" hanging just two feet from me.

My second Manhattan emboldened me to take a closer look at the painting. The very clear signatory in the bottom right hand corner of the artwork was "T. Royston, 1929." That the work was completed in 1929, the year Royston died, created an eerie ambiance which was accentuated by the bar's dim lighting. It was undoubtedly the last painting he did before he died. Definitely, this was a little spooky. But, I still couldn't believe what I was seeing. Finding a major work by an incredibly famous artist is the stuff of dreams.

"Do you like the painting?" I heard someone behind me ask.

I turned to see who was speaking to me. It was a patron at the far end of the bar. Besides the bartender and me, he was the only other person in the place. He sat in a shadow and I couldn't see his face very clearly.

"Yes, I like it very much," I replied.

"Night Sky in Williams" was a beautifully done study of a one block area in downtown Williams and the star filled night sky. It featured the Hotel Ammerman, Rundell's Ladies Wear, and Munson's Haberdashery. Only one person was shown in the painting, almost as an afterthought, it seemed. It was a woman in a black, sleeveless cocktail dress. She was wearing black high heels and standing in the glow of a bright street light which sat four feet above her atop a pole. Short black hair accentuated her attractive face and bright red lips. She held a small pistol in her right hand.

"May I buy you a drink?" he asked.

I told the man I was only half way through my second Manhattan, but he insisted. The bartender set a third drink in front of me.

"Do you like Royston?" the man asked, his face still obscured by the shadow.

"Yes, he was a brilliant painter," I replied. "I noticed this particular piece is less severe than some of his others," I further commented. "I mean, this painting is more of an ethereal study rather than a critique of man's abuse of the planet and the beauty of Earth."

"Yes, that is true," he replied. "But, it is also meant to be revelatory."

"It sounds like you have an interest in art," I replied.

The bartender was watching us, carefully listening to the conversation.

"Oh I paint a little," the man said, shifting somewhat in his chair and inadvertently revealing more of his face. Though his mouth was small and refined, his lips were full, determined looking. I noticed his hands. They were small and distinctive, appearing skilled, if one could actually assess artistic ability by looking at a person's hands.

The man was wearing a faded blue denim shirt and worn khaki pants. His shoes were spattered with various colors of paint. "Yes, he's artistic looking," I decided, as I took another sip of my third Manhattan. It went down very nicely and the bartender efficiently replaced the empty glass with a filled one.

"In what way do you mean the painting is revelatory?" I asked.

The man chuckled and the bartender smiled. "I mean the painting contains the answer to a mystery," he replied.

"It's my turn to buy" I said to the man at the end of the bar, who was himself somewhat mysterious. But, he had already paid.

"Sir, I continued, "you have bought two drinks for me and I don't even know your name.

"I'm the owner of the painting you're admiring," he replied.

Although the man's eyes and forehead were still hidden by the shadow, as he leaned forward I could see more of his face. He looked vaguely familiar.

"You're very lucky," I said. "There are many people who would pay a great deal of money for that painting. How and when did you happen to come to own such a beautiful work of art?" I asked.

"I painted it," the man replied.

I was puzzled by his answer, thinking it was bar talk and intended to be humorous. But then he rose from his bar stool and stood looking at me.

"My God!" I gasped to myself. Shocked and horrified, I watched Thomas Royston walk slowly toward me.

He stopped next to where I sat and pointed at the painting. "You see the woman in the painting?" he asked. "She is the one who killed me. You are not sitting here by some happenstance, but because I brought you here."

Aghast, I could only listen to Thomas Royston as he spoke.

"I'm going to give you this painting but there is a condition attached," he said. "You must confront this woman and tell her you know she killed me. I will take care of the rest. Do we have a deal?" he concluded.

"Yes, of course," I replied, still so astonished I could hear myself breathing. "But, who is the woman?" I asked.

"She is my wife," he answered. "She lives on her ranch north of Williams."

"But, why did you choose me?" I asked. "Why do you want me instead of someone else to confront your wife?"

"Because you appreciate my paintings and, more than anyone else, you really understand my work. I want you to have my last painting, "Night Sky in Williams.""

Thomas Royston took the painting from the wall and handed it to me. "It is yours," he said.

I took the painting from him. Although I never imagined I would own a Royston, I was quite disconcerted at the manner in which I had acquired it. If this was really happening and not some kind of bizarre dream, there was something frightening about making a bargain with a dead man. I smiled at him and he smiled back.

"Thank you," I said.

Abruptly, it became very dark and cold and my right shoulder was aching. My head was throbbing with pain and I couldn't seem to focus my eyes. A moment ago, I was sitting in a comfortable saloon talking with a dead artist and now I was lying outside on some concrete steps. As I sat up and my eyes adjusted to the darkness, I was horrified when I looked toward the Hotel Ammerman at the top of the concrete stairs. All the windows were boarded up and weeds and trash were scattered around the beautiful front gardens I saw when I checked in. The hotel had obviously been closed for a very long time.

I was astonished and perplexed at what had happened.

I was having a drink at the bar with the artist Thomas Royston and he gave me one of his paintings. But it was 1947 and Royston had died in 1929. It couldn't have happened but it seemed so real. As if to confirm what must have been a drunken delusion, when I looked around for the painting it was gone.

I didn't know how I got to where I was or even where I had gotten drunk. I distinctly remembered checking into the Hotel Ammerman and drinking at the Chief Wise Eagle Saloon. The next thing I knew, I was lying on the concrete steps in front of the abandoned hotel.

I struggled to stand up. Luckily, across the street was a place called Cleary's Boarding House. I would get a room there and try to sleep this off. But I doubted I would get much rest. I was completely unnerved by what had just happened to me.

As I feared, I got very little sleep. I kept trying to figure out what had occurred the night before. The next morning I got up, showered and drank a cup of coffee. As I went out the front door of Cleary's Boarding House, I looked across the street and saw the abandoned and badly neglected Hotel Ammerman. Still quite disconcerted and upset, I shook my head as I walked to my car.

I sat there in the car for a long while, still trying to sort out the events of the night before. There was no doubt in my mind I had checked into the Hotel Ammerman, had drinks in the bar with the long dead Thomas Royston and had his painting in my hands.

Then I remembered Royston asked me to stop at his wife's ranch north of town. He also asked me to confront her as she was his murderer. Although I didn't intend to "confront her" as he put it, I decided to find out where the woman's ranch was located and stop and see her. I was still badly shaken up but I thought I might find some relief to my torment if I could talk to the woman. I went back into Cleary's Boarding House and got directions to the ranch owned by Royston's wife. It was a short drive and I arrived in about fifteen minutes.

It was still early morning when I walked up the front porch steps and knocked on the door. No one answered. I knocked several times but still, there was no answer. The heavy wooden door was open and I put my head close to the screen door to peek inside.

"Is anyone home?" I shouted.

There was no reply. Again, I pressed my head to the screen door to look into the house. It was an ordinary living room with a couch, several chairs and a coffee table. But I was suddenly stunned. Hanging on the back wall of the living room was "Night Sky in Williams."

I grasped the handle of the screen door. It was unlocked. Ignoring caution and a growing apprehension, I pushed the door open and went inside, then slowly walked across the living room to the painting.

I stood there studying the breathtaking artwork, marveling at its beauty and depth. The passion of the artist was evident in each stroke of his brush. Although every one of Royston's paintings was well documented, neither I nor anyone else was aware he had ever executed this particular piece.

It was then I heard a female voice to my right. "Do you like the painting?" she asked, restating the same words Thomas Royston had said to me the previous night.

As I turned toward her, I realized I was facing the woman depicted in the "Night Sky in Williams." She was noticeably older and dressed in more casual clothes but her short black hair and bright red lips confirmed her identity. There was one other thing which was the same. In her right hand she was holding a small pistol, and it was pointed directly at me.

"Who are you and what do you want?" she asked.

"I am an art critic and a great admirer of your husband's work," I said. "I am particularly interested in the "Night Sky in Williams. It is a beautiful work of art."

"Thomas sent you" she responded conclusively. "He

told me someone would come to avenge his death."

"How could he do that?" I responded. "He has been dead for eighteen years."

That the woman was holding a gun caused me considerable fear. More terrifying however was that she didn't appear to be at all reluctant to shoot me. She raised the gun and pointed it at my head. I knew I should run but I was so frightened I couldn't move.

"Thomas is one of those kinds of people who just won't leave you alone," she replied. "So don't lie to me. I know he somehow communicated with you from the grave."

"That's impossible," I replied, although I knew she was correct in her presumption.

"You're lying!" she snapped venomously. "The very fact that you know the name of the painting is "Night Sky in Williams" is proof that you're lying," she added. "Only Thomas and I knew of the existence of "Night Sky in Williams. The only way you could have known the name of the painting is if he told you."

She aimed the gun more deliberately, getting ready to pull the trigger.

"No, please!" I begged. "Don't shoot me. You are wrong about this."

"Goodbye, Mr. …….., how funny, I don't even know

your name," she said coldly.

As she took final aim, her expression stiffened to a ruthless glare and her left eye closed. Her hand clenched the gun tightly. My blood ran cold and I knew I was going to die.

She started to squeeze the trigger but decided to move closer to make sure the bullet found its mark. Still frozen with fear, I could only watch.

As she stepped forward, her foot caught under the carpet and she tripped. She fell forward and, as her body struck the floor, the gun fired with a loud cracking noise. She lay motionless and face down, a pool of blood slowly forming under her head. The gun was still in her hand.

For a moment, I stood there looking at her lifeless body. Then I raised my eyes to look at the "Night Sky in Williams." But the painting was gone, leaving only a bare wall where it had hung. I ran across the living room and threw the door open and bolted down the steps to my car. I quickly drove the car down the long dusty driveway to the main road and tuned left to begin my drive north to the Grand Canyon.

As I drove away, I looked into my rear view mirror to make sure no one saw me leave or was following. But the back window was blocked by a large rectangular object covered with brown wrapping paper. I didn't remember putting anything into the back seat of the car and I pulled the car to the side of the road and got out.

Opening the rear door, I reached into the back seat and pulled the wrapping paper from the rectangular object. Sitting before me was "Night Sky in Williams."

Gremlins Over Page

The B-26 Martin Marauder was in a fatal high-speed dive and losing altitude fast. If Mary Jane Kicheloe couldn't pull the twin engine bomber back to level flight, the three women on board would be dead in less than a minute.

What had started out as a routine flight from the Martin factory at Middle River, Maryland had abruptly become a fight for survival high over Page, Arizona. Mary Jane and her crew were WASP's, Women Airforce Service Pilots recruited in World War Two to transport airplanes.

The B-26 normally carried a crew of seven in combat however it only required a team of three to ferry the airplane across the country. Besides Mary Jane, there was a co-pilot and a navigator/radio operator. It was early 1943 and their job was to fly airplanes from the factory to military airfields.

The B-26 was difficult to fly and inexperienced pilots had a high accident rate. Although Mary Jane was one of the best WASP pilots, strange, unexplainable things were happening on this flight. She had no idea how to handle them. They were headed to Long Beach Army Airfield and their present position was fifty miles northeast of Page, Arizona. They were flying at 18,000 feet. That's when the trouble started.

Navigator/radio operator Billie Jacoby saw a misty shape float through the bomb bay area. She moved to the cockpit to ask pilot Mary Jane about the phenomenon. Both women dismissed the mist as not important. As they talked however, the bomb bay doors began opening and closing wildly. Billie went back to take a look. She quickly did a manual override and the bomb bay doors slammed shut. Billie wondered if the mist she saw had anything to do with the bomb bay doors going crazy.

Then the airplane started "wagging," that is, the tail of the airplane began swinging from side to side. Mary Jane pushed hard on opposite rudders but couldn't get the big bomber under control.

"Billie," she yelled, "go back there and see what's going on."

Billie quickly moved toward the rear of the plane and stuck her head into the dorsal turret, which was normally manned by a gunner with two machine guns. She looked back at the tail and was horrified.

"Mary Jane," she called, "there are two little men playing seesaw on the tail, pushing it from side to side."

"What?" Mary Jane barked into the intercom. "You have your oxygen mask on Billie?"

"Mary Jane," she screamed, "they are out there on the tail trying to crash the plane! There are two little men with beards and stocking hats dressed in red and green outfits and wearing black boots. They can't be more that a foot tall. And they're laughing. They know they're scaring us to death."

"Joan," Mary Jane shouted to her co-pilot, "get back there and see what's wrong with Billie. She's hallucinating."

Joan unhooked her seat belt and quickly moved toward the rear of the plane. Billie was still looking out the dorsal turret window toward the tail of the aircraft.

"Get out of there and let me take a look, Billie!" Joan yelled excitedly.

119

The engine noise made it difficult for the women to hear and the tail swinging from side to side made it hard to keep their balance. As Joan stuck her head into the dorsal turret, she couldn't believe her eyes. It was just as Billie reported. There were two little men with beards literally pushing the tail toward one another causing dangerous control problems for the pilot. And, just as she had also said, they were laughing.

"Mary Jane," Joan called into the intercom, "we've got gremlins on board. There are two on our tail and that misty shape Billie saw must also have been one. We've got to land the plane immediately."

Mary Jane had heard reports from the combat areas about gremlins on airplanes. The mischievous little men misaligned bomb sights, caused engines to fail, and made instruments go haywire. She thought that the term "gremlins" was a catch-all kind of term for imaginary wee people pilots blamed for unexplained problems. She never thought they were real. However, she did recall that some pilots swore they actually saw gremlins and described them exactly as Billie and Joan had.

"Good Lord," she said, they're real."

"Mary Jane," Joan called from the dorsal turret, "traffic

at three o'clock."

Mary Jane had already seen the four fighter planes which were probably based in Phoenix and on a training mission. They were flying east in tight formation. Suddenly, however, the right wingman peeled his airplane off from the group and headed straight for the B-26.

"What is he doing?" Mary Jane yelled to Joan. "He's coming right at us."

"Why doesn't he turn?" Joan screamed back, as she climbed back into her seat on the right side of the cockpit.

"He's got to see us," Mary Jane shouted, "but he just keeps coming."

"Hold on Billie!" Mary Jane yelled into the intercom. "We're going into a hard dive."

But the fighter plane was diving too, still coming right at them. The gremlins were intent on bringing the B-26 down and were somehow causing the fighter plane to steer right at their bomber so it would crash into them.

"There must be gremlins aboard the fighter too!" Mary Jane exclaimed. "Pull up, you idiot!" she screamed into the mike, hoping the fighter pilot was on the same radio frequency. "He can't control his airplane either! Pull up!" she shrieked again.

But it was to no avail because the gremlins were calling the shots. Mary Jane saw the fighter pilot bail out just before his plane crashed into the right side of the B-26 fuselage, leaving a gaping hole which ran diagonally from top to bottom on the airplane's right side. Apparently only the fighter plane's wing hit their B-26. However, Mary Jane was now struggling to bring the big bomber out of the dive.

"Pull hard, Joan!" she screamed. "Pull hard with everything you've got!"

Both pilots had their yokes pulled back all the way but the plane wouldn't level off. It was diving directly toward the town of Page, Arizona. Not only would the three women in the crew die, but many people on the ground would also be killed.

Mary Jane and Joan looked at each other. The engines were screaming and air was roaring through the huge hole in the right side of the plane. The town of Page was coming at them fast. If they didn't pull the plane out of the dive in the next critical seconds, they would crash into the small city. But the two pilots couldn't pull the plane to a level flight attitude.

"This is it!" Mary Jane screamed. "We're going in!"

"No!" screamed Joan. "I don't want to die!"

"Do something, Mary Jane! Billie screamed into her ear.

The town was so close they could actually see people walking around. They would crash into the town in a few seconds and a lot of people would die.

Suddenly, the nose of the airplane responded to the two women who were still   pulling hard on their yokes. As the nose of the airplane began to rise toward the horizon, the "G" forces pinned the women to their seats. The engines were on full power and roared loudly as the airplane strained hard to stop losing altitude. Then the "G" force decreased to normal as the plane reached the level-off point. The plane was flying over two hundred miles per hour and was no more than forty feet above the ground.

"Look out!" Mary Jane screamed as the plane roared past the town's water tower, just missing it by inches.

The left wing clipped the top of a tall tree and Mary Jane pulled back slightly and the elevators shifted the plane into a gentle climb. They didn't climb far however. Joan pointed out the Page airport and Mary Jane banked the B-26 in a hard left turn and headed directly for the small air field. They landed the plane quickly and shut down the engines.

When they climbed out of the airplane, they were astonished at the damage the bomber had sustained. The tail was beaten up and had large dents in it. The left horizontal stabilizer was bent upward. And the gash in the right side of the airplane was so large, Mary Jane was surprised the airplane wasn't cut in half.

As the three women stood surveying their wrecked airplane, they heard voices and hysterical laughter. Under the tail section of the B-26 were three little bearded men dressed in red and green. They were pointing at the still very rattled women and laughing at them. And suddenly, they disappeared. The gremlins had struck again.

Note: In 1943, Allied Headquarters in North Africa set up Gremlin Detector Squads to deal with "gremlin events" as they were called. Gremlins were especially prevalent in the North Africa Theater as well as Great Britain. Numerous air crew members reported actually seeing the "little people" described above.

Tusayan Spirit Trail

Milton Dunbar reached into the darkness for his carbine. "Got it," he declared   silently, as his right hand grasped the rifle's wood stock. Slowly, cautiously, he pushed his bedroll aside with his left hand while simultaneously moving the gun upward and across his chest from its customary spot by his right side. He grasped the barrel in his left hand, its steel ice cold even though the gun lay in the warmth of his bedding.

"Petey," he whispered sharply, but not loud enough to be heard by anyone or anything else, he hoped. "Petey, wake up. There's somethin' out there stirrin' up the cattle."

But Petey, the oldest cowhand in northern Arizona, didn't answer. "He should have hung up his spurs long ago,"

Milton thought to himself.

"Wake up, Man!" Milton called in a louder whisper. "The cattle are restless, Petey. We gotta take a look."

Earlier that day, the two men had left the tumble-down, clapboard hotel in Tusayan to hunt for strays in the pine forest to the north situated between the town and Grand Canyon. They worked for the Breckenridge ranch seven miles southwest of Tusayan, and picking up strays before winter came was an annual ritual. They never rounded up more than half a dozen cows each year but the foreman sent them out for two weeks every fall just the same.

"It's gotta' be a mountain lion," Milton thought. "Or maybe it's a black bear."
Whichever, he wanted no part of either. Milton always kept his boots on when he slept outdoors just in case he had get up quickly, as in times like this.

He was on his feet, creeping low as he moved toward the barely visible lump on the ground that was Petey under his blanket. Milton had to be careful because once when he roused the sleeping man, Petey came close to shooting him. It's never a good idea to wake up a sleeping cowboy, particularly an old one who doesn't hear or see too well.

The night was pitch-black, the scarce light from the stars and quarter moon diminished by thick branches of the dark, tall pines spiraling above them. As he reached forward and gently grasped Petey's shoulder, the only sound Milton could hear was the movement of the four cows stamping restlessly in the makeshift corral of rope strung around pine trees.

Milton shook Petey but couldn't get him to wake.

"Petey," come on!" he whispered, more loudly.

He shook the sleeping man again. "Wake up Petey," Milton whispered impatiently.

But, there was no response from the old man.

"Dang it!" Milton whispered. "I'll do this myself, Petey, but I'm taking your rifle so you don't accidentally shoot me."

Milton reached under the bedroll to take the man's gun. The old man had a firm hold on it. The cows were making more noise. Whatever was bothering them was getting close. He moved his hand down the length of the gun to find Petey's hands and pull the weapon from his grip.

But he recoiled in shock when he touched the old man. Petey was colder than the steel barrel of the carbine.

"You're dead, you old crowbait!" Milton hollered, ignoring whatever danger was lurking in the disquieting gloom of the forest.

His fear was replaced by anger. He knew he should be mourning Petey's death but with the present situation, he was mad at the old man for dying and leaving him   alone.

"Dang it all!" he muttered toward the cows. The sound of his voice brought some meager comfort, making it seem that someone else was there with him and whatever animal was prowling out there might be scared off.

But it was not to be. The four frightened cows were mooing loudly and grunting now, crowding hard against the corral's rope perimeter and jumping to get past it. Holding the carbine tightly with his left hand, Milton pulled the lever down, then up, to set the bullet in the chamber. Suddenly, the rope snapped and the terrified animals burst from the corral and stampeded toward the south.

They thundered past Milton, leaving him standing alone in the foreboding forest with a dead man and two hobbled horses. Milton looked around slowly, straining to see through the darkness. The forest was so gloomy and lightless he didn't think he could even see someone standing next to him.

Earlier when they set up the campsite and corral at the edge of the small, open meadow, Milton hadn't noticed anything unusual. But now, as he looked more closely at the patch of land and the tall pine forest surrounding it, he could see a long, straight strip of night sky through the treetops on each side of the clearing. It was as if someone had cut a trail through the treetops. But as he thought about it, he remembered he and Petey had followed what they thought was a natural path through the trees as they searched for the lost cows. But he could now see that the long cut through the forest was straight and even, created for a specific reason.

Though he knew ancient Indian tribes lived in the area a thousand years before, this strange route through the tall pines frightened him. And although Petey had been his friend, the man's dead body added to his growing unease.

Suddenly, he felt someone touch his right shoulder. He spun around and pointed his carbine at whoever was behind him. He gasped as he recognized Petey standing before him. But it was not the Petey he knew. Milton was certain that Petey was quite dead. Besides, he could see this Petey in the thick darkness. There was a faint luminescence to him, a sort of soft, silver glow. And his body had a misty quality about it, like you could stick your hand right through it.

"Hello, Milton," this new Petey said.

"Hi," Milton replied fearfully, knowing he was talking to a ghost.

"You are standing on the trail of the dead," the apparition said. "After people die, their spirits follow this trail to leave the earth."

"I'm leaving this place right now, Petey," Milton said.

"Yes, you are Milton," the apparition replied. "After people die, their spirits follow this trail to leave the earth".

It was then that Milton looked down at his own body. There was a faint luminescence to him, a sort of soft silver glow. And his body had a misty quality about it, like you could stick your hand right through it.

And Milton knew he was a ghost.

Misunderstanding in Jerome

Edward Blixbee was an accountant working in Jerome in 1917. The copper mines were operating at full capacity then. Edward had been skeptical about taking the job in Jerome because it was known as "The Wickedest town in the West" due to its many saloons and brothels.

Today was a rare day off work and he headed to Molly Flanagan's Saloon. He had been there before but on this visit something did not seem right.

The people in Molly's on this day were not the usual clientele nor were they wearing current style clothing. He thought they were dressed in period costumes, like people from year's past. He had seen people dressed this way in old photographs.

He walked across the room to the heavy wooden bar with the big mirror. An unfriendly bartender with a handlebar mustache set a mug of beer in front of him.

"Here you be, Archer," he said.

Edward was planning to drink whiskey but, in view of the bartender's disagreeable demeanor, he decided not to argue.

"You want anything else? Archer," the bartender asked rudely.

"My name's not Archer," Edward replied.

"Yeah okay, Archer," the bartender answered with a disgusted look.

Edward noticed the piano music stopped and people had become silent. Edward lifted his mug and took a sip of his beer. The bartender had moved away from him and in the bar's large mirror, Edward could see all eyes were watching him. Holding his beer, he turned to survey the crowd. They looked very upset.

"You got a lotta nerve comin' back here, Archer," a voice hollered.

"My name's not Archer," Edward protested.

That pronouncement only riled the crowd. Edward decided to make a hasty exit. As he turned to set his beer on the bar, his eye caught the calendar hanging on the big wooden side post of the mirror. The date displayed was July 19, 1867. Suddenly bewildered and fearful, he threw a dollar bill on the bar and turned to leave.

A loud thud and stabbing pain across his lower jaw rudely informed Edward he was in a bar fight. The fist from a second man landed in his stomach, doubling him up and causing him to collapse to the floor. He couldn't catch his breath to protest, and what seemed like one hundred boots began kicking his body. He passed out quickly.

"Hey, Mister," a man's voice yelled, "are you okay?"

Edward opened his eyes, rather his right eye, as the left one was swollen shut. He tried to answer but his lower lip was split open and painful. The man helped him up.

"What on earth happened to you?" the man asked.

"They beat me up," Edward answered.

"Who beat you up, Mister?" the man replied.

"Everybody in the place beat me up," Edward said.

The two men walked over to the bar. The man, apparently the bartender, gave Edward a wet rag. When Edward looked around the barroom, not a soul was in the place.

"Where did everyone go?" asked Edward.

"What do you mean, Mister?" the bartender asked.

"I'm the only one here. We don't open for another half hour.

How did you get in here anyway?"

"But the place was full of people just a few minutes ago," Edward replied.

"Mister, there ain't nobody here but you and me. I sleep in a room upstairs and just came down to open the place and found you," the bartender said.

Perplexed, Edward looked at the man across the bar from him. Then he noticed the calendar hanging on the big wooden side post of the mirror. Today's date was displayed. It was July 19, 1917, exactly fifty years later than the calendar he saw earlier.

"You know, Mister," the bartender said, "you're a spitting image of Archer Willis, the man in that photo hanging on the wall over there. He's the man who killed the bar's original owner, Molly Flanagan, in 1867. Vigilantes dragged Archer out here and hanged him fifty years ago today. So, we have happy hour all day.

Edward glanced at the picture and was immediately shocked. He was looking a   portrait of himself.

"My god!" he exclaimed solemnly, "I was nearly hanged by a barroom full of ghosts."

GHOSTS OF INTERSTATE 90 Chicago to Boston by D. Latham

GHOSTS of the Whitewater Valley by Chuck Grimes

GHOSTS of Interstate 74 by B. Carlson

GHOSTS of the Ohio Lakeshore Counties by Karen Waltemire

GHOSTS of Interstate 65 by Joanna Foreman

GHOSTS of Interstate 25 by Bruce Carlson

GHOSTS of the Smoky Mountains by Larry Hillhouse

GHOSTS of the Illinois Canal System by David Youngquist

GHOSTS of the Niagara River by Bruce Carlson

Ghosts of Little Bavaria by Kishe Wallace

Shown above (at 85% of actual size) are the spines of other Quixote Press books of ghost stories.
These are available at the retailer from whom this book was procured, or from our office at 1-800-571-2665 cost is $9.95 +
$3.50 S/H.

GHOSTS of Lookout Mountain by Larry Hillhouse

GHOSTS of Interstate 77 by Bruce Carlson

GHOSTS of Interstate 94 by B. Carlson

GHOSTS of MICHIGAN'S U. P. by Chris Shanley-Dillman

GHOSTS of the FOX RIVER VALLEY by D. Latham

GHOSTS ALONG J-35 *by B. Carlson*

Ghostly Tales of Lake Huron **by Roger H. Meyer**

Ghost Stories by Kids, for Kids by some really great fifth graders

Ghosts of Door County, Wisconsin by Geri Rider

Ghosts of the Ozarks *by B Carlson*

Ghosts of US - 63 by Bruce Carlson

Ghostly Tales of Lake Erie by Jo Lela Pope Kimber

GHOSTS OF DALLAS COUNTY	by Lori Pielak
Ghosts of US - 66 from Chicago to Oklahoma	By McCarty & Wilson
Ghosts of the Appalachian Trail	by Dr. Tirstan Perry
Ghosts of I-70	by B. Carlson
Ghosts of the Thousand Islands	by Larry Hillhouse
Ghosts of US - 23 in Michigan	by B. Carlson
Ghosts of Lake Superior	by Enid Cleaves
GHOSTS OF THE IOWA GREAT LAKES	by Bruce Carlson
Ghosts of the Amana Colonies	by Lori Erickson
Ghosts of Lee County, Iowa	by Bruce Carlson
The Best of the Mississippi River Ghosts	by Bruce Carlson
Ghosts of Polk County Iowa	by Tom Welch

Ghosts of Interstate 75	by Bruce Carlson
Ghosts of Lake Michigan	by Ophelia Julien
Ghosts of I-10	by C. J. Mouser
GHOSTS OF INTERSTATE 55	by Bruce Carlson
Ghosts of US - 13, Wisconsin Dells to Superior	by Bruce Carlson
Ghosts of I-80	David Youngquist
Ghosts of the Cumberland River	by Bruce Carlson
Ghosts of US 550	by Richard DeVore
Ghosts of Erie Canal	by Tony Gerst
Ghosts of the Ohio River	by Bruce Carlson
Ghosts of Warren County	by Various Writers
Ghosts of I-71 Louisville, KY to Cleveland, OH	by Bruce Carlson

Ghosts of Ohio's Lake Erie shores & Islands Vacationland   by B. Carlson

Ghosts of Des Moines County   by Bruce Carlson

Ghosts of the Wabash River   by Bruce Carlson

Ghosts of Michigan's US 127   by Bruce Carlson

GHOSTS OF I-79   **BY BRUCE CARLSON**

Ghosts of US-66 from Ft. Smith to Flagstaff   by Connie Wilson

Ghosts of US 6 in Pennsylvania   by Bruce Carlson

Ghosts of the Missouri River   by Marcia Schwartz

Ghosts of the Tennessee River in Tennessee   by Bruce Carlson

Ghosts of the Tennessee River in Alabama by Bruce Carlson

Ghosts of Pamlico Sound   by Linda June Furr

GHOSTS OF THE BLUE RIDGE PARKWAY   BY LARRY HILLHOUSE

Mysteries of the Lake of the Ozarks   by Hean & Sugar Hardin

GHOSTS OF CALIFORNIA'S STATE HIGHWAY 49   *BY MOLLY TOWNSEND*

Ghosts of La Salle County   by Joan Kalbacken

Ghosts of Illinois River by Sylvia Shults

Ghosts of Lincoln Highway in Ohio   by Bruce Carlson

Ghosts of the Susquehanna River   by Bruce Carlson

Ghostly Tales of Route 66: AZ to CA   by Connie Corcoran Wilson

Ghosts of the Natchez Trace by Larry Hillhouse

Ghosts of Kentucky's Country Music Highway   by Bruce Carlson

Ghosts of Arkansas Highway #7   **by Gary Weibye**

Ghosts of the Land Between the Lakes   by Larry Hillhouse

Ghosts of Lake Norman   **by Linda June Furr**

To Order Copies

Please send me _____ copies of *Ghosts of the Grand Canyon* at $9.95 each plus $3.00 for the first book and $.50 for each additional copy for S/H. (Make checks payable to **QUIXOTE PRESS**.)

Name _____

Street _____

City _____State _____ Zip _____

QUIXOTE PRESS
3544 Blakslee Street
Wever, IA 52658
1-800-571-2665

— — — — — — — — — — — — — — — — — —

To Order Copies

Please send me _____ copies of *Ghosts of the Grand Canyon* at $9.95 each plus $3.00 for the first book and $.50 for each additional copy for S/H. (Make checks payable to **QUIXOTE PRESS**.)

Name _____

Street _____

City _____State _____ Zip _____

QUIXOTE PRESS
3544 Blakslee Street
Wever, IA 52658
1-800-571-2665